LIBRAM MYSTERIUM

VOLUME TWO

Libram Mysterium Volume 2 is published by Pulp Mill Press.

Cover art by Christopher Conklin.

Trade Paperback Edition
Published in 2014

ISBN: 978-0-9936324-1-9

Pulp Mill Press
www.pulpmillpress.blogspot.ca

LIBRAM MYSTERIUM

VOLUME TWO

EDITED BY SEAN P. ROBSON

CONTENTS

THE PISCINA
BY GARNETT ELLIOT...9

LE DIEU PERDU
BY JOSH GRABOFF...19

IN MY TIME OF DYIN'
BY ALASDAIR CUNNINGHAM.....................................29

THE PALM READER
BY MATTHEW BOTTIGLIERI.......................................43

WORMHOLES
BY MARY QUIJANO...49

THE DANCERS ON THE WALL
BY ALEX J. CHRISTY...59

TRACKS
BY LISA BUCKLEY...73

CHEAP VODKA SAVES THE WORLD
BY S.M. OKEYB...81

THE DRINKER OF SOULS
BY SEAN P. ROBSON...89

FORWARD

Even before I was finished laying out the first volume of Libram Mysterium, I knew I wanted to make the second volume a themed issue, dedicated to pulp-style horror reminiscent of the works of H.P. Lovecraft, Clark Ashton Smith, Robert E. Howard, William Hope Hodgson, Algernon Blackwood, and other great horror writers of the early twentieth century.

As much as I love horror stories, I dislike the label 'horror.' It's a loaded term that promises to evoke feelings of intense fear in the reader, which is pretty hard to do, and it sets a story up to fail by its very definition. Horror is also a nebulous term. It is usually used as a convenient way to categorize a sub-genre of speculative fiction, and within the literary field it tends to be contemptuously dismissed as mere 'genre fiction.' But what we think of as horror spans all genres, it explores the most visceral aspects of human psychology and probes the dark heart of the human condition. It is one of the most important ways for us to explore who we are, and we've been telling these types of stories for as long as stories have been told, including one of the earliest works of fiction, the Mesopotamian Epic of Gilgamesh. Consider these literary masterpieces: *Lord of the Flies*, *Heart of Darkness*, *1984*, and *A Clockwork Orange*, just to name a few. They are horror stories, each and every one, but you will never see them shelved in the horror section of any bookstore or library. Horror forms the foundation of all literature, and it is far too nebulous a concept to pigeon-hole with a genre label. Instead of asking, 'what is horror,' we might better ask, 'what isn't?'

Personally, I prefer to use the term 'macabre fiction,' or 'dark fantasy' to distinguish stories with horrific elements in any given genre. The macabre stories included in this volume run a gamut of horrors: historical and contemporary, supernatural and psychological, and of course a smattering of existential cosmic horror to boot. They're all here, ready to pick at the crusted scabs on your soul, so come in and make yourself at home for, in the words of Clive Barker, "we have such sights to show you."

Sean Robson
October, 2014

THE PISCINA
GARNETT ELLIOT

"Oh come now, what's with these long faces 'afore the first course is even served? Is my hospitality so dreadful you must comport yourself as if at a funeral—and a poor one at that, without a lively host of gladiators and slaves about to fall before the sword? Steward, more wine for these dormice!"

Vettius paced the tessellated floor, wringing his hands as he spoke. He had thick pink fingers to go with his ample face, fleshed and unlined as a well-fed child's. Spittle flew with his lament. Behind him, a pair of stout centurions stood at guard.

The three guests sat among Vettius's purple cushions as if surrounded by wolves, their jaws taut, eyes bright and wide, avoiding contact with each other and the covered platters set before them only moments earlier. Each had been whisked away from various parts of the empire, seized in the night and brought here, to Vettius's secret villa, atop a remote island in the Ligurian Sea.

The steward, a young Phrygian freedman, moved among their silver cups, deftly pouring a purple wine so dark it seemed black. When none of the guests were quick to drink, Vettius scowled.

"Do you think I'd have you brought all this way, just to poison you?" He snatched up one of the fresh-poured cups and drained it to its lavender dregs, before hurling the vessel to the floor. "Now drink! Fortunata, you will lead us with the toast."

One of the guests, a plump woman wearing the garments of a senator's wife, her dark hair pinned back in Eastern fashion, managed a pained smile. "But I'm not the host, Lord Vettius." She nodded to the two men sitting nearby. "And it still escapes me, why exactly I've been brought here, in the company of these other distinguished persons."

"Well said, Fortunata. The answer, in a word, is 'love.'" Vettius rolled his eyes for the briefest moment. "Your emperor, in his boundless compassion, has decided to show mercy to you all. He forgives your individual transgressions—you each know of what I speak—and in lieu of some messy state execution, has willed you here, to feast in grand manner at my estate while you pontificate upon your errors."

"We all know the nature of these 'feasts,'" said a second guest, a lean man with rope-like muscles under a soldier's simple tunic. He leapt to his feet. "We're to be punished in some gruesome manner so as to appease Nero's sensibilities."

"Sit down, General Buitoni," Vettius said.

"Better to fight, I think." His eyes stole to a golden knife set alongside a platter.

Vettius nodded to the centurion on his left. Up came a pilum over a muscled shoulder, before it blurred a short distance and struck the floor inches from Buitoni's reaching hand. He drew back as if struck, a cautious expression settling over his face.

"Very good, general. And let me assure you, there's an excellent chance at least one of your company will survive this night unscathed, if my commands are followed to explicit instruction." Vettius folded his arms. "Now sit."

Buitoni sat.

The third guest, an older man grossly fat where Fortunata was merely plump, raised a hand to speak. Golden bangles clashed on his wrist. "I have yet to understand the reasons for my being brought here. You spoke of 'transgressions,' though I can recall no personal crimes against the state."

"Ah, Gordanius, that's where your memory fails." Vettius resumed his pacing. "You will recall the recent conflagration that took half of Rome? And the emperor's appeal, to all those merchants dealing in marble, timber, masonry, and in your case, lead?"

"I gave him a fair price," Gordanius said, his cheeks flushing, "and he sought to cheat me..."

Vettius raised a finger. "Do not use that word in discussions involving our beloved emperor. Nero is the embodiment of fairness."

Buitoni snorted. "He played his lyre atop the Palatine while Rome burned. I have it on good authority."

"I heard he started the fire in the first place," Fortunata added, "to make room for that monstrous palace he's building."

"Silence!" Vettius managed a stern expression, though sarcasm seeped into his voice like honey oozing from a comb. "I will not listen to you impugn that first among Romans, my brave cousin Nero. So perhaps he is overly sensitive to slights. Perhaps his taste in architecture bankrupts an empire. No matter! I am sure his mother, Agrippina, will in due time re-exert her influence, and the emperor will again suckle wisdom from her teats... but I digress. I must call the toast, as Lady Fortunata reminded me. Steward, charge this spent cup, and bring a fresh one for me."

When the Phrygian had obeyed, and all the vessels brimmed with purple wine, Vettius lofted his own cup. "Ave Nero, on whose favor we all depend, dubious as it may be." He drank deep. The guests showed hesitation, but when the leftmost centurion's hand crept to the hilt of his gladius, a trio of cups flashed in the torchlight.

Vettius clapped his hands. "Now to the courses. Steward!"

The cover atop the first golden platter was snatched away. Beneath lay a heaped assortment of pilchard, mussels, and small carp, ringed by oysters and cockles in the shell, all fragrant with wine sauce and wisps of rising steam. The meal would seem appetizing enough, even luxurious, save for the color of the fish. Both the carp and pilchard were a sickly white, pale as bleached bones.

"Harvested from my own fish ponds," Vettius explained. "As to their flesh: this villa was built atop a much older Etruscan ruin, and beneath the foundation stretches an ancient limestone cavern, fed by both freshwater springs and inlets from the sea. There I raise my stock in near-lightless conditions, with the resulting anemic appearance."

Fortunata's lips curled in disgust, and Buitoni drew back from the platter, nostrils flaring. But Gordanius, undaunted, snatched up a long-tined fork and speared a pilchard, which he thrust in his mouth.

Vettius brightened. "A gourmand, I see. Well, I think you'll appreciate the second course. You other two must eat as well, or I'll have my soldiers force it down your gullets."

Fortunata and Buitoni grudgingly consumed shellfish, while Gordanius feasted with smacking gulps. Fortunata, in the process of worrying open an oyster, let out a startled cry.

"What is it, dear Lady?" Vettius said.

"This shell—it's been inlaid with a gold letter 'F'."

"Has it now? 'F' for Fortunata, perhaps? Open it and see."

She used a small knife to split the valve, but her look of expectation turned to panic when she saw what was inside. The shell tumbled from her nerveless hands, disgorging its contents atop a cushion. It was a finger severed at the second knuckle. A gold band set with a garnet encircled the pale flesh.

Vettius shook his head. "You recognize the present to your lover, Albanus? Frankly, I can't fathom how you keep track of all your bed-mates. The popular tally has it over two hundred."

"Slander," Fortunata said, recovering some of her composure. "Ceaseless lies. I ignore such talk."

"Your husband bears the shame less skillfully. You can imagine the jibes he's had to endure from his fellow senators, married to a woman who maintains a harbor's traffic between her legs."

"If my husband weren't so busy with his painted boys..."

"Discretion, dear Fortunata, is the soul of proper infidelity. You've made the horns on your husband's head so many times he complained directly to Nero. Thus, your presence here. And now, I think it fitting you feel the weight of those horns yourself. Are you familiar with the Cretan legend of Pasiphae? No? Well, you'll become acquainted soon enough. Guards!"

A second pair of armored centurions came clanking into the banquet chamber, their faces impassive. They seized Fortunata with rough hands and pinioned her between them. General Buitoni tensed as if contemplating rescue, but a glance at the first two centurions, standing at the ready, seemed to cool his warrior's spirit. Fortunata shrieked outrage as she was hauled from the chamber.

Gordanius and Buitoni traded looks. Vettius, acting as if nothing untoward had occurred, nodded to the attentive Phrygian. "Time for the second course."

Another golden cover lifted, accompanied by groans from the two guests. An octopus lay atop the platter. Albino, like the fish, but tinged with the pink of a mild steaming, and still very much alive. Limpid eyes stared up at its would-be devourers. Suckered tentacles squirmed.

"You can't be serious..." Buitoni said.

Gordanius, prompted perhaps by Fortunata's rough treatment, seized a knife. The octopus's bloated head roiled an angry scarlet; black ink came bubbling out from beneath, in the manner of a dying man voiding himself on the battlefield.

"Courage now," Vettius said. "Here stands the test of a true epicurean. Cut!"

Teeth clenched, Gordanius lifted the knife and hacked down with a butcher's urgency. The blade bit into the yielding flesh of a tentacle, causing sallow juices to spurt. Mute, the octopus let its chameleon skin bear protest, rippling from seething red to purple, and then a pained, pale yellow. Its mournful eyes followed the tip of Gordanius's knife as he brought the still-quivering flesh to his mouth. He chewed.

"Well," he said after a moment, "it is fresh..."

"Bravo! Have another taste, but mind you leave a hero's portion for good Buitoni."

With less hesitation than before, Gordanius raised the knife to claim a second piece. But he halted. Furrows appeared on his brow.

"Is something wrong?" Vettius said, unable to hide a smirk.

"There's a roll of parchment, wrapped in one of the tentacles."

"So there is." Vettius paced closer to peer over the merchant's shoulder. "And a bold seal set upon the parchment, with the letter 'G.' Dare you open it?"

Gordanius licked his lips. "I think not."

"Oh, come now. I'll read it for you." Vettius snatched the roll from the octopus's grasp. He shook free drops of ink and hot water before breaking the seal. "The words have been smeared, but I think I can still discern them... why, it is addressed to you, Gordanius, and in Nero's own hand . . . he makes reference to your punishment, citing another story of far-off Crete. The legend of Talos. Please tell me you know something of it, unlike our ignorant Fortunata."

"Talos?" Gordanius's chin quivered. "A giant made of bronze, if I remember correctly."

"The very one. A gift from the Gods to Minos, forged with but a single vein running from head to ankle. In lieu of blood his great heart pumped molten lead. Does that suggest anything to you, oh tight-fisted peddler?"

"I'm afraid not."

"Your fear is likely well-founded." Vettius stepped back and clapped his hands. "Guards, attend!"

Another pair of centurions appeared. They hefted the merchant with effortful grunts, moreso due to his weight than the quality of his struggles. Buitoni made no move to intervene. In his flailing, Gordanius kicked over the octopus tray and sent the creature rolling. Vettius watched with a dour expression.

"Well, I suppose I can't insist you eat it now," he said, after Gordanius had been dragged away.

Buitoni squared his shoulders. "You mentioned earlier that one of your guests might stand an 'excellent chance' to survive the night. May I assume

I've won that honor?"

"How so?"

"By being the last."

"Ah, well..." Vettius's grin showed a hint of dimples. "I may have temporized a bit, holding out that hope. But don't act surprised, Buitoni. Did you really think that your crimes, of all those bandied this evening, would warrant forgiveness?"

The general shrugged. "It was only two legions."

"And in Hispania, no less. I daresay I could've managed better against those Iberian thugs myself. In any case, I now present the third course."

He shouldered the Phrygian aside and lifted the cover from the final golden platter himself. It was empty save for the reflection of the banquet room, and the eerily distorted faces of Buitoni and his host.

"I don't understand," the general said.

Vettius replied by slamming the heavy gold cover against the base of the general's neck. It pealed like a crude bell, and down went Buitoni.

"In your case," Vettius said, "I opted to forego all this monogrammed nonsense. It's the piscina for you."

Consciousness returned to Buitoni with a curdling scream, though it had not, thankfully, come from him. Blinking, he found himself in a cavern of impressive girth, lit by shoals of oil lamps. His wrists had been bound behind him with leather thongs. The two centurions who'd been attending Vettius now pressed close on either side, their hands grasping him from beneath his armpits. Evidently, they'd been carrying him for some distance, while his mind swam through darkened nether-realms. The back of his head throbbed where he'd been struck.

"That woke you, did it?" came Vettius's honeyed voice. Buitoni turned his head—not without pain—and saw the madman, grinning like an imp. Half his face was lit by guttering lamp light, the other by a hellish molten glow. "Mark you, Buitoni, the fate of Lady Fortunata."

He nodded towards a nearby section of cavern, where the senator's wife lay prone. Astride her bulked a giant bull cast from bronze, glowing red-hot. A great fire must've been stoked within its bowels. Fortunata's eyes bulged, her mouth gaped in frozen agony, but no further screams escaped her mouth. The bull's searing ardor had already claimed her life.

"Disappointing," Vettius said, "that she expired so quickly. You missed their brief courtship. Ah, but over here we're just in time to witness the punishment of miserly Gordanius."

Buitoni refused to look in the direction indicated, gazing instead at his feet. A pair of hands seized him by the temples and forced his attention to a far corner of the cavern, where Gordanius, shackled flush against a wall, was being fitted with an enormous funnel, thrust into his mouth. Chains clattered; slaves hoisted a cauldron of bubbling lead above the funnel. At a nod from Vettius, the cauldron tipped. Steaming liquid metal poured down into the merchant's throat, squelching his cries. Bound limbs danced a jig as Gordanius's already expansive gut swelled and burst, spilling a mixture of gray lead and yellow fat. Mercifully, smoke rose in a cloud and shrouded the rest of the merchant's passing.

"Also a bit too quick, that," Vettius said, "though Gordanius was much more generous in death than life. He's given us enough tallow to make a score of candles."

Buitoni swore. "Of all the barbaric... you make the cruelest Gaul seem gentle as a nursemaid."

"Withhold your compliments until you've seen my piscinari. Come."

Vettius led the small procession out of that terrible chamber, heavy with the smells of hot metal and burning flesh, down an adjoining tunnel. After a brief period of darkness they emerged into a second cavern, less expansive than the first. Natural pools riddled a mosaic-strewn floor. Lurid blue-green phosphorescence lit the waters, so that a myriad of scuttling, swimming, and swirling shapes could be seen. All bore the sickly mark of albinism. Buitoni glimpsed a pool choked with octopi, their pale tentacles roiling the surface. He thanked the Gods Gordanius's flailing had spared him a taste of their flesh. Not that the sentiment brought much comfort.

"Attend to this pool here," Vettius said. "Observe how the waters appear placid."

He gestured towards a pool of middling depth; clear, and devoid of repulsive shapes. But when Vettius dipped his toe and sent out ripples, hundreds of grayish-white forms came squirming from niches along the walls. They had the sleek, undulating bodies of eels, and a disc-shaped mouth radiating with serrated teeth. Most were the length of Buitoni's forearm. They arched and craned and twined their horrible maws above the surface of the water, like a bed of flowers seeking the sun.

"My lampreys," Vettius said, with the same pride as a father observing his sons at play. "I've starved them for a fortnight. Too much longer and they'll turn on each other, but your presence will forestall that, my good general."

15

The centurions dragged Buitoni to the pool's edge and made ready to hurl him in. He took a deep breath... and laughed.

"What's this?" Vettius said. "Your disciplined mind finally breaks? Gods, but I've not gotten much satisfaction out of you otherwise, tonight."

"This farce has played out much too long," Buitoni said, speaking not to Vettius but the thin-legged centurion on his right.

"Indeed." The soldier removed his crested helmet with a flourish. The lank blond hair, blue eyes, and stubbled beard thus revealed struck all present, for it was the same countenance gracing a thousand marble busts throughout the empire, and all silver denari as well.

"My lord," Vettius said, dropping to his knees in sudden obeisance. "I did not know..."

"Nor were you supposed to," Nero said. "Word reached me, cousin, of a certain churlish attitude on your part, when speaking of the emperor. Tonight I've gleaned the truth myself."

"But lord--"

"I task you with the disposal of special prisoners, and this is how you repay my sinecure? With sarcasm? Mocking my leadership, my tastes in architecture--even questioning the strategy of my generals, like stalwart Buitoni here?"

Vettius's chin stopped quivering for a moment. "Stalwart? He lost two of your best legions."

"This is exactly what I'm talking about." Nero shook his head. "Even now, to my imperial face you show obstinance. Buitoni's two Hispania legions had grown mutinous under a certain sub-commander, who urged a march on Rome. But the general craftily maneuvered them into an ambush. Without his intervention I might be facing an open revolt at this moment."

"You do me honor, Lord Nero," Buitoni said.

"Merely a recitation of the facts." To Vettius he said: "And you, of all people, should understand how fragile a thing my self-esteem is. I am first and foremost an artist, with an artist's painful sensibilities, thrust into the cold world of politics..."

"I abase myself a hundred times, great Nero." Sweat was beading on Vettius's upper lip. "I will quit this fabulous villa and lead an austere life, hereon."

"Oh, I doubt that." Nero motioned to the remaining centurion, who drew his gladius and cut Buitoni's wrists free. The two then seized Vettius by his plump limbs.

"I had been contemplating allowing you the dignity of an asp," Nero continued, "or eating a pound of salt with a golden spoon. But for that comment about my mother's teats, you'll feed the lampreys yourself."

"No! Not my pets! That's fratricide, Nero, and too monstrous, even for—"

But Buitoni and the centurion had already dragged Vettius to the pool's rim. They tossed him in without ceremony. Ravenous lampreys reared and attached themselves even before he'd struck the water. Vettius disappeared with a noisy splash, to come thrashing back up moments later. Wriggling shapes covered him like a carpet. He fought lustily, tearing a few of the mouth-discs from his skin, pulping a half-dozen slimy bodies in his grasp. But more lampreys came boiling. They affixed themselves to his forehead, to his eyes, their near-translucent skin pulsing red as they gorged.

Nero watched with nary a grimace. "Cruelty begets cruelty. Never forget that, Buitoni."

"I won't, my lord."

"I suppose I should have this villa demolished. If word ever got out of the practices here, some of my short-sighted critics might think me excessive."

"Just so."

"As for Vettius, I propose we make a feast of these lampreys after they've glutted. Nothing fattens like aristocratic blood. Then I'll have my cousin's remains cremated, and the ashes scattered through the sewers of Rome."

Buitoni nodded, his stomach already quailing at the prospect of such a feast.

"Do I detect some hesitancy on your part?"

"No, Lord Nero."

The emperor's watery blue eyes narrowed. "What was that crack you made, about my playing the lyre while Rome burned?"

"Just repeating a falsehood, in order to convince Vettius of our ruse."

"Hmmph. Everybody says that about me. I would hate to think history remembers Nero for that one rumor." After a moment, he added: "I but touched the lyre's strings, Buitoni. The muse was upon me, and the tempo of the crackling flames all but demanded a song..."

"Truly, you have the soul of an artist."

They waited for the lampreys to finish.

LE DIEU PERDU

JOSHUA GRABOFF

Sit, if you please, monsieur. You've that look about you—you want to hear of my part in the Mazarin affair, hm? Don't start so, that's what all who come to my fireside are after. But I think I give 'em something quite different, something they weren't looking after. I've a fine chocolate, if you like. Keep a good supply whenever I can, buy it up from the ships that come in at Calais through my agents. Have a cup. I assure you, I have plenty and my coffers won't be exhausted in my own lifetime, so there's no worry on that count.

It's all quite fine, is it not? You would hardly believe that my father lost our fortunes in the '20s before the war put us at blows and he nearly sold our titles as well. Our debts kept mounting until I saw no other choice but to put on arms and armor and serve Richelieu. I didn't really understand the causes of the damn thing, much as the old Comte tried to explain it to me, but I didn't need to comprehend the ins and outs of the Bohemian Revolt or any of that other Protestant nonsense. I know that Richelieu thought we were in awful trouble, with the Hapsburgs surrounding us on either side and poised to gobble up France, so to hell with co-religionists and we threw in with those Calvin-loving rebels.

So when I came back to Paris in the spring of sixteen hundred forty seven in the year of our lord, I'd had my fill of Protestants. I was overjoyed to hear Mazarin was planning on forcing those Hugenots left in France to convert upon my first visit to the salons that year, though the word was that the Edict of Nantes must remain ironclad. And it was said that King Louis was equally hard on 'em, or more so, and he was nearing his majority. Three cheers for our roi, I thought. If I could have anticipated the effects revoking the Edict would have on France... but I was young, and stupid, and full of vigor. I hadn't achieved the great wisdom I was to find in later years.

I had no small fame in those days for my exploits, though the first time I saw a man die I must admit I nearly choked on snotty tears and I never developed a taste for the battlefield. The smell of powder was enough to shiver me right down to my heels. Not that I was a coward, you see, for I still knew my duty. My so-called bravery at the front traveled on winged feet like Mercury. Here was the man who'd stood up to German cannon, urged his fellow sellswords on, and followed the Cardinal to victory against the Hapsburgs. The salons were all abuzz with my name. You, being young, can't imagine what it was like. You see an old wrinkled man, caked with powder and hiding behind his titles and a lifetime of roguery. That's not who I was back then. I implore you, monsieur, to imagine me young and virile, stupid and headstrong. That was the boy I had become. I do not say man, for though I'd already had my fair share of women, I was not yet in any sense a man. That came later, with Monsieur C—.

We met at the salon of Charles de Neufville de Villeroy, Marquis of Villeroy et d'Alincourt. He was Grand Quartermaster of France and a Chevalier of the Holy Spirit, and also old as sin by then. But he ran a most excellent salon in his house in Paris which was frequented by all the great minds of the nation at that time. You'll have undoubtedly heard that l'Hôtel de Rambouillet was the center of all social life in Paris; if it was, l'Hôtel de Villeroy was as its orbiting wanderer. I came at the invitation of some friend or other who was in the Marquis' good graces. Everyone found it quite commendable to have me—what with being something of a celebrity in those days. I was no slouch at conversation either, I can promise you that. I held converse with some of the finest statesmen and poets of our time.

My memory of meeting him is one that I shall never forget in all my long years. I was seated in a window seat overlooking a garden... no, I don't recall where exactly the residence of the Marquis was. Paris was different in those days, you'll excuse me for saying so. More refined and somehow more brutish as well. It was already autumn by then, and the wind was exquisite cold. My breath was frosting the pane and most of the leaves were already off the trees. There was a Lenten feeling to the air, and even the priests were starting to behave more soberly at gatherings. That's how you could tell that Christmas was coming, you know; the closer to it, the less they drank right until the mass was over and then they fell back into their cups, all a-clatter.

By that time I had become somewhat tired of the Paris set, I must confess. I was bored of their chattering, which always seemed to revolve in circles without ever coming to conclusions. They drank too much, and they fucked far too often for my liking. I've never shied away from the libidinous pleasure, you know, but after a while it just seems excessive. I come off as a prig now, I'm sure, but let me tell you—I had my fare share of belles across the city! But truly by then the life of hedonia and libertinism had begun to exhaust me and I was looking to settle and marry well. Perhaps I could parlay my skills into a commission for the crown and earn myself a living through the army. I thought I would quite like that, as long as it didn't take me to the front again and away from the civilized comforts of France.

It was in such a mood as this that Monsieur C— found me. He has knack, for knowing when people are at their weakest points, non? He approached me and I admit that for a moment I thought I saw a double of myself: a young, handsome, dark-haired man with pale green eyes that trembled like emeralds bedecked with dew. But as he drew nearer the illusion vanished and I saw he was far my superior in looks and grace. He wore a finely slashed doublet of gold and deep maroon breeches that ended in a cavalcade of golden tassalry just above his high boots. He had the natural fluidity about his movements that spoke of long training at the épée.

"And you too," he asked me, "find this gathering tedious, yes?"

I snorted and sloshed the wine in my glass. I can recall the feeling of the warmth spreading through me, realizing that I was already somewhat tipsy, perhaps because I had taken so little for luncheon. "How can you tell, monsieur? Surely I thought it well disguised." I spoke sarcastically, of course, for I had my back to the twittering women and expounding philosophers and had been focused on the gardens and their leafless greenery for quite some time.

"We-e-e-ell," he said, and he joined me upon the seat. He didn't make eye contact, just sat beside me and examined the horizon. "If I had wanted to discuss the price of joint-stocks I would have visited a grocer's."

"And if I'd wished to debate the likelihood of the Trinity, I'd have taken orders," I added with a smirk. Of course, no one would be quite so harebrained as to debate theology of that level at a salon, but it served my point and Monsieur C— laughed heartily. I look back now on that genuine and pleasant belly laugh and wonder if he meant it. Probably not. Appearing to care deeply and truly was one of his myriad gifts, and probably the chiefest of them all.

I decided that I liked the company of Messr. C— and he evidently liked mine as well. I told him where I had my lodgings, but he never returned the favor. I didn't think it odd then, but I wonder now where he lived during my time in Paris. Never once did I see a dormitory, a room at an inn, or anything even resembling living quarters for Messr. C—. But that never seemed to matter and I only realized it when I looked back on those years in light of the things that were still to come. C—, as I began to call him, was expert in finding the finest soirées and the most important houses.

We fell in with one another like old amis, drinking and whoring together once the slow circular conversations of the salons became too much to bear. We were bon amis together as though we'd known each other our whole lives. C—felt like my oldest and greatest friend, though I'd only known him for a few weeks. We were inseparable, he and I; wherever I went he came as well. Wherever he went, he invited me along. It all seems so hollow now, looking back on it, a sham put on for my benefit. He was too friendly, and we got along too well. I couldn't tell at the time, of course. Who can? It was a little like being in love. You may find that strange, perhaps, but I don't. Not after what I've seen. C— could make you feel that way, like the rest of the world had simply stopped existing.

Best were the times when we were snidely mocking the cream of Parisian society to their faces. Le reine was still regent in those days, but Mazarin had the rule of the nation—and for good reason. But everyone was slurring him in their parlors, as though they had a better grasp of foreign policy than our own Italian genius in the Louvre. While the peasants outside were growing more and more discontent with the crown and Mazarin particularly, the fops were dancing and laughing at the plight of the Bohemians. So we sneered at them and made them into jokes in their own salons.

Society began to talk about us. Those hellions, those rapscallions we became. Yet somehow, C— always got us into the chic gatherings anyway. I thought we'd be blackballed, but people actually seemed to like us. One night at the Marquis' we each put on the airs of one of Paris' famous socialites: the Mme de Sévigné, who'd just fled the city to get married to Henri de Sévigné a few years prior. She was a nasty letter-writer and some of her claptrap against Mazarin's niece, Mme Mancini, had just come out in society. I flounced across the room, dashing off mimed letters one after the next in an orgy of laughter while C— pretended to be Mazarin himself, fretting over what they portended; "Ees-a thees-a plot?" he gargled in perfect imitation of the statesman. We'd become social satirists, the toast of the town.

One evening, when I'd gotten quite a lot of champagne and port down, C— convinced me to imitate the abbé d'Aubiniac, François Hédelin, who I did a passable impression of. We were at l'Hôtel de Rambouillet, which was obviously not the best choice of venue for the occasion. Indeed, even Mme Sévigné was there, scowling at us as though we'd killed one of her prized pets. In a sense, we probably had; her reputation was a shambles, at least for a few weeks. Anyway, what I didn't know then was that Richelieu himself was watching when I, as the abbé, pretended to grapple and fuck C— in the ass while he pranced about proclaiming himself the duc de Fronsac. You maybe don't know enough about France back then. You see, Fronsac was one of Richelieu's nephews and Hédelin was his tutor.

Of course no one said anything, they just let us make complete asses of ourselves. That night, when we were wandering drunken through the city, C— laughed and told me that he'd known Richelieu was there all the time. "I saw him from the minute we stepped in!" And then he laughed, that stupid, ugly, beautiful charming laugh that threatened to draw me in and disarm me. But I wasn't to be disarmed. No, I was furious, seething. My chances at advancement had just been shot in a single go. I railed at him, I nearly cuffed him. I don't know what would have happened if I hadn't restrained myself. He might have killed me. I didn't know then that he could have, just like that.

"I'm going home," I said sullenly. He laughed at me and assured me everything would be alright. Just come for another drink, ami, just one more. "I'm going home, damn it," I replied, to show him I was serious.

Didn't I just? He took me by the shoulders and looked into my boozy eyes. "You think they didn't deserve it?"

"Deserve it? You've scuttled my hopes for a captaincy, you god-forsaken fiend!" I railed. "The cardinal! In front of the cardinal, we as much as said that his nephew was raped daily by that bloody lawyer!"

"Come with me," he said, and he grabbed me roughly by the arm and began to walk in a very determined manner away from the Île de la Cité. I wanted to fight him, but his grip was iron-strong. His fingers bruised my flesh and I glared occasionally at him to let him know I wasn't having a good time any longer. He didn't seem to care, for his face was all pale and trembling with anger.

He took me into the darker quarters of the city. When I asked where we were going, he refused to answer. It was clear that he knew his way—he took no turn at random, but every step was purposeful and determined. At last we slowed. I knew where we were: one of the roughest patches of Paris in our day. "Why are we here?" I demanded of him. He just piloted me into an alleyway and pointed at the lean gentilhomme at the far end. Some nob getting sucked off, it seemed to me, until the moon caught his face. By God! It was the abbé d'Aubiniac, may the Lord strike me down if I'm mistaken! And the little figure attending to his cock was a boy of no more than twelve. Some street urchin. "How did you—?"

C— cut me off. "I know everything that goes on this city, ami. You just don't understand that yet, to your loss."

Over the next few days, C— took me to gambling hells and showed me how to make money. Not that I could replicate the feats he pulled off. He simply told me where to place my silver or when to draw cards and I did as he said. My money began to rapidly multiply. "In exchange for losing you Richelieu's favor," he explained. All very well, save for the mysterious manner in which my sous seemed to come pouring in. But you don't look a gift horse in the mouth, unless it's brought to you by Greeks.

I used the money to buy better lodgings, better clothes, and better perfumes. C— complimented me on my taste often, and we bought a shared stake in a brothel off the Rue de Temple, ironic as that may sound to you now. We continued to attend parties and salons. Though I wanted to reduce the number of shows of "witticism," C— would have none of it. We burned our bridges as fast as they were made, lampooning the great and small alike.

Around this time the crowds were starting to get ugly. Winter was in full swing, and the price of bread had come down again thanks to Mazarin's price controls, but people still complained about his taxes. They didn't understand, I suppose, that the taxes were what enabled the cardinal to release food and subsidize the city granaries and flour. It didn't matter, for no one at the salons seemed to care in the slightest.

I was sleeping off a terrible gueule de bois from the night before when C— had plied me with three bottles of port, a jaunt in our own bordel, and a midnight hack ride at high speeds around the city. The driver was mortified but we just laughed and laughed, the freezing Parisian air stripping our throats dry as we leaned from the windows to howl at the moon. C— came to my lodgings the very next afternoon and roused me from my stupor. I cursed him and threw a mug at him, but he only laughed and got me to my feet. "You remember Mme de Sévigné?" he asked me. Of course I did, I told him, how could I not? After our little joke, the Madame had scuttled three engagements of mine to meet fine young women.

"You know I was trying to settle down," I told C—, to which he only grinned fiercely, like a baboon.

He tapped me on the forehead with the silver grip of his stick cane. Now they're all the rage, but back then I think he was one of the only people who had one. "Her husband has come to the city, and I think it's time we take a look at his parlor."

I didn't know what he meant, because of course it was still light out and there would be no salons opening until later in the day. Besides which the

24

Mme de Sévigné didn't keep a salon of her own—she preferred visiting others. But C— led me towards the Île de la Cité again and I realized that we were going to the townhouse the Sévigné's owned along the Rue Saint-Séverin. "We'll never get in there," I grumbled, pointing out the footmen, the gate, the high spikes of iron along the walls, and the well-tended garden. Once again, C— just smiled. It was then that I think my love of him peaked. I'm not ashamed to say that I felt a burning urge to kiss him on the mouth, and damn be to the consequences. I didn't, of course. Don't look at me that way, young man. If you'd known C—...

He took me around back, weaving through the side-alleys until we came to a servant's entrance near the stables. "She parades her marriage around, speaking of her husband as though he were a golden Adonis," C— said. "And meanwhile butter wouldn't melt in her mouth." He gave me a puckish glance, the twinkle in his eye that spoke of deep cunning and danger glimmering. "But we'll see about that, eh, mon ami?"

The servants appeared to know him, and let him in without a second question. We crossed through a back courtyard and entered the Sévigné house through the kitchens. Old women and young men alike bowed before him and greeted him with a deferential air. The head chef, a fat middle aged creature with dugs down to her waist, gave us both toasted almonds to eat and nearly fell over herself fawning on him. I was a little jealous, I'll admit. How did he know these people? He'd barely been out of my sight in months!

We walked through the twilight rooms of the house, passing drawn curtains and slender shafts of light as though they were a forest of silence. He pointed his cane at the staircase that swooped down into the main foyer. "Now we shall see the loving couple for what they are, hmm?" At the top of the stairs there was a grotesque trophy of the kind that Henri de Sévigné liked to keep. He was a hunter, both with bow and pike, and he apparently killed fifty or more Bretagne harts each year. There was a great stag's head right at the top of the stairway, uncouthly mounted upon the wall, its ugly little mouth partly open. I don't know what he was thinking or what person in their right mind would ever deign to be entertained in a house with such a gory keepsake on public display... but there it was, right against the fine Damask-style wall papering.

Quietly as church mice, we crept up the stairwell. C— stayed at its head, but pointed with his cane to the place where I should go and listen. There was a door part-way open, a pool of winter sunlight spilling from it. On soft feet, I slunk towards it. I could hear the murmuring of voices, one male and one female, on the far side. As I drew nearer, they resolved into words. "I can't help it, woman. It's not my fault!"

"Oh, truly? Is that it Henri? It's my fault then?"

I glanced back at C—. He gestured for me to peek inside. I did as he bid me, and I saw the elegant spread of the Marquis' bed, the unbolted windows, and the Madame de Sévigné sitting on the bedcovers. Henri was propped up against the crown of the bed, his cock flaccid in his Madame's hand. She was partly undressed, her breasts free and her gown part-way torn. I nearly choked at the sight. "I can't say this has ever happened to me before we were married," Henri said.

"And yet it seems every night and afternoon's occupation, no matter what steps we take," his wife replied acidly.

I wanted to flee, but I knew if I moved quickly I would draw attention to myself with the noise. I gave C— an imploring look. There was something strange about the way he stood, all outlined in the dim shadows of the hall. It took a moment for me to realize what it was and then: spreading horns. He was framed just so against the head of the stag. He seemed to tower nearly nine feet in height, and from his brow there sprouted the grim shadows of the stag's horns. The illusion vanished as I made my way toward him, but the whole scenario left a sour feeling in my gut for days.

Of course, C— hadn't just brought me there to give me a glimpse of the home life of the Madame. No indeed, for he began cajoling me just the following day that I must make use of our new found knowledge. "She has interrupted your pursuit of a bride," he said. "So now you must interrupt her marriage. She clearly isn't being satisfied in the boudoir."

I knew better than to ask him how he'd found that secret out. At the time I thought he must have half the servants of Paris on his payroll. There was no accounting for the things he seemed to know, otherwise. Ha! If only that had been true. But then, I wouldn't be so stinking rich now, eh? And I certainly wouldn't have been able to make myself a Duke.

At his urging I pursued the Madame de Sévigné until I had her in a cloak room. She purred for me, and C— fed me just enough information that I would always know what to say or do to keep her close. I was beginning to resent his interference just a little bit; it had started in good fun, but it seemed he was intent on being my guide through life, and each time he drew back the curtain to show me something sordid I felt a little part of myself drain away. The final straw came when he offered to let me take money from the coffers of Notre-Dame. "My God, C—! Does your wickedness know no bounds? Those are men of God!"

That was the end of our relationship. He scowled at me, snarled. "You think they're men of God, do you? Is that what you think? I'll show you what those men are!" I didn't want him to, I told him as much, but that night he dragged me all the same to the cathedral. I half expected it to be locked, but the doors sprang open to his touch. Damn, I thought, I wish he would stop! Just for a moment halt his relentless attack on everything around him. Society was corrupt, yes, everyone knew that! But it was still a place where people had to live—where I had to live. And he was making it nigh unlivable for me. I wanted to be ignorant, I realized then, I wanted to ignore the evil truths that made up the underpinnings of my station. Did I tell you that he showed me a slave market? No? Before that, a week or so before, when I was still bedding the Mme, he took me to a slave dock where Africans and some Europeans were chained up and sold off the coast to be bound for the Americas.

That night he led me through the maze of pillars, naves, aisles, and back rooms of Notre-Dame de Paris, I felt like I was going to be sick. The most beautiful building in France, le gloire de Paris, he was going to turn into shit around my ears. "You think these are men of God!" he scoffed again. His voice echoed through the sleepy cathedral but he seemed unafraid of being found out. "You still, after all I have shown you, believe that the world is worth caring about! Ha! You're a fool. Come this way. Come on! I will show you what everything is built upon. The beautiful stained glass stands in a mire of shit, mon ami."

He led me at last to a back room where a big ledger was kept. He opened it and showed me the lists of payments the cathedral had been making. I couldn't believe it—at the behest of Cardinal Mazarin, the canons of Notre-Dame had been engaged in the most heinous graft I had ever seen. There were a great many respectable nobles on the lists, investments in some south seas trading company, payoffs to mayors and comtes, and worst of all—slavery. The canons of Notre-Dame had assisted Mazarin in purchasing interest in a slaving company. I felt as though I was going to be sick.

"What's wrong with you, C—? You're no man! No man could bare to look the world in the face like this. So tell me!" My voice grew in volume until I was near shrieking. "Tell me why you would do this!"

"Pfffaugh," he said, shaking me off like a dog throws off a louse. "I thought you were different. I thought we shared something; that you could be made to understand."

It was then that I realized everything. C— drew himself up and I saw the shadow of those horns sprouting from his forehead. How could he have known the things he knew? How could he have charmed those servants in the household of the Sévignés? There was only one answer. "You are the Devil!" I gasped.

"The Devil!" he cried. "I have been here since before the Devil was born! I am Paris, I am the Boatman. Who are you, damn you? You have sucked from my teat, enjoyed my company, and done my bidding—who are you? I have not made this filthy city. You made it. Men like you, men who think and act and pretend at goodness. I should strike you down!" He raised his stick cane and the spars of stone in the ceiling cracked and leaked dust. He seemed stronger here, as though the very ground of the Île de Cité gave him strength. I cowered. "You ungrateful creature! Look at the ugliness you have made for your own glorification! Look at the edifice you have raised on bones and misery! This is your so-called civilization! This is your so-called France!"

He struck me and I blacked out. The blow should have killed me. I woke in my apartments. I never saw C— again after that, nor heard even a word of him spoken in the salons. Shortly, my invitations stopped coming and I was no longer one of the highlights of French society. But C— had taught me many things about human nature, yes? He had shown me where the levers were, and how to work them. I used his lessons well, my friend. That chocolate you're drinking; do you think I would be able to afford it if I had not been as devious as my old friend, Monsieur le Diable?

I hear they have found an old pagan relic in the earth beneath Notre-Dame. Some kind of obelisk? And it has a horned man dancing upon it, non, engraved in the stone? Yes, that is he, my one-time friend. The beautiful Monsieur C—. So, now you know why I refuse to visit Paris. But you are young and still full of life. You know, you remind me so much of myself in those days—all false fronts and the façade of courage. I have a good feeling about you. No, no, don't draw away. You know my coffers are damnably full and I have access to the keys that open every door in Paris. A few words in the right ears... Ah, yes. Come closer and sit by the fire with me. Perhaps you like my company more than you care to admit. Perhaps I like yours as well. Yes, you remind me of myself, all those years ago. Don't look so shocked, my boy. We share something, you and I.

IN MY TIME OF DYIN'

ALASDAIR CUNNINGHAM

When he wasn't out on the road he was drinking and thinking, sitting on his porch overlooking a hard-pack desert bordered by the brown smudge of mountains, way out west. He just couldn't take the constant humidity of the southern states anymore. Always too hot, too muggy; it irritated his arthritis and made him feel like a catfish caught inside a wet burlap sack. That's why he lived in a house on the dry, dusty wings of the Mojave Desert; it was good for his bones, and all that light and space that surrounded him really helped him to create.

Lyric was a blues-man, and like all blues-men that have gone before he had a dark streak, and not just a sliver either; Lyric had it in spades. When he sang, his voice was low and furtive and alligator stealthy. You could imagine it sliding off a muddy bank and into a swamp. Surprisingly, given he smoked two packs a day, it could also soar; flapping high on leathered pterodactyl wings, crackling and spitting like lightning or frying black cat bones.

He sang of evil and heartbreak and feckless women spawned by the devil himself. Occasionally, he sang of love, but more often of lust. He wailed about murder, shrieked over jealous lovers, and rasped on what people would really do for money.

Lyric played the guitar. A down-on-its-luck Gibson Les Paul held together with duct-tape and venom. She was malice-black and he could make her sing... make her squeal... make her moan; his playing was fluid, seminal, with a strong dark undertow. He christened her Midnight, and proclaimed she was the only woman who'd never stepped out on him.

Lyric, always dishevelled, unshaven, and in black, was tall, thin, and stooped from countless years of cheap motel beds and cramped tour buses. He looked like the town undertaker in a cowboy movie, complete with sallow skin and an ill-temper.

He drank nothing but black coffee, spirits, and beer. The last time he drank a glass of water was back in '54, and only because he mistook it for neat vodka. To add to his woeful diet were the drugs: a pharmaceutical cornucopia, and the sniffing, popping and spiking began the moment he opened his eyes. Lyric didn't really wake in the morning, not in the normal sense, Lyric came to.

Despite his Bacchanalian debauchery, his latest album, Storm Warning, was riding high in the charts. He was booked to play eighty-two sold-out performances from New York to L.A., and all points in-between. Life was good for Lyric, he felt like he had arrived at last, like Homer back from his odyssey.

They were somewhere on the edge of the desert playing in a small club when he saw her standing at the back of the audience drinking him in, as if his every word was the air that she breathed. The spotlight panned slowly over a sea of sweating faces that all looked the same to Lyric—a perfect cross-section of society—except for hers. Hers was different... feral almost, and it gave Lyric pause.

The light, soft and warm, seemed to snag on her hatchet face and when they made eye contact, she winked. Nothing unusual about that, she'll be throwing me her panties next.

Her pallid hair blazed under the spotlight, but her eyes were a fevered, jaundice-yellow, which glowed balefully from under thick arachnid eyelashes. She smiled at him, sharp and cold and cruel, reminding Lyric of the kind of damage you could do with a straight-razor on unsuspecting flesh. It was more of a bleeding gash than anything, and it sent a jolt of fear through the aged performer. Her teeth were yellow and discoloured, and her gaunt fallen face was wan and sickly. She was the epitome of a meth-head.

Then her jaw began to work, up and down, stretching, like a snake before it swallows a rat. A forked tongue emerged and probed the air, licking the unreachable parts of her leering face. He could see the crowd ripple around her, like the rock that parts the stream. They were avoiding her presence, as if they sensed something was wrong in their midst.

There was a jarring noise in his head like a badly tuned radio; he tasted blood in his mouth. His fingers slipped off the fret board causing a burst of wild, jagged feedback to screech from the amps stacked behind him. He turned from the audience to regain his composure and when he looked back she was gone, replaced by the face of a bearded fan wearing a Led Zeppelin T-shirt. The faintest whiff of sulphur lurked just beneath the sweet scent of marijuana that came rolling in off the crowd like a fog.

30

Shit, what's that about? I must be higher than I thought... but he wasn't, and he knew it. Maybe it was a mask? Or an acid-flashback? It has to be some shit like that, he thought desperately. What if that shit was real... like the groupie from hell? Lyric was trying to convince himself it had just been a trick of the light.

After the gig he asked the others if they saw her, the girl with the ashen hair and bloody smile. They looked at Lyric as if he had finally lost it.

Perturbed, he retired to his dressing room for a drink and a smoke before leaving for the next town.

On a table, next to his unopened bottle of Scotch, was a withered black rose with a note attached. He had a sneaking suspicion he knew who it was from but hoped he was wrong. The same sulphurous smell coiled in the corners of the room. The handwriting was thin and spidery and read,' Cryin' won't help you... Prayin' won't do you no good...'

He sat down, staring at his expression in the harsh light of the makeup mirror. Shut your mouth, Lyric...you're drawing flies he thought. The rose was significant to Lyric; it had been the name of his debut album. Lyric heard warning bells in his mind.

He poured himself a stiff drink, sat back, and wondered what it meant. If it was designed to get his attention it worked. He tapped the note against his teeth. Maybe she was just a stalker with a deep sense of the macabre. It wouldn't be the first time I've encountered one of those. My type of music really brings out the crazy in people...or maybe it's just nerves, there's a lot riding on this tour for me and my band. But none of that washed with what he had seen, or what he had thought he had seen.

The following evening at the Long-Pig Palace, Lyric stood hunched over, crow-like, under a spotlight rapping to the crowd; while Bart—his long suffering roadie—changed a broken guitar string. He was keeping a weather eye out for the girl, praying last night was just an isolated incident, but he had requested extra security on the floor and in the wings just in case things went south.

"There is a certain sound a city makes," he said, addressing the audience, killing time between the songs, waiting for his axe.

"A low class hum, a drone, with subtle peaks and troughs, ebbing and flowing with the rise and fall of the sun... but at night, when the lights come on and the stars are out, it mellows... fading from frenetic to the sublime hiss of...pure... white... noise..." Lyric laughed, it sounded low, guttural, like a well that's waiting to swallow a child.

The audience clapped and hollered; they loved to hear him ramble. The beauty of Lyric's fame was that even when he wasn't singing, they still found him captivating.

Bart, now back on stage, thrust Midnight into Lyric's hand. He had the next bit of stage patter ready when he saw her. She was standing closer this time, about twelve rows from the front, just on the cusp of where the footlights met the dark. She laughed and danced and gave Lyric a little wave. His prepared stage rhetoric slid from his mind. He fell silent. A crimson spotlight swept the audience dipping them in blood; they looked like a flock of sacrificial lambs at slaughter. Silence blanketed the hall.

The band waited. The audience waited. No one moved. Except for her; she swayed her hips from side to side like a practised seductress, running her long thin fingers sensually over her body as she moved to her own beat. Lyric stared. Large drops of sweat beaded his forehead and slid into his eyes making them sting.

He took a handkerchief from his back pocket and wiped his face. He blinked repeatedly, squinted out at the expectant audience; and then she was gone and he was left staring sprung-mouthed and trembling at some middle aged house wife out for a good time with her friends.

A polite cough from John, the drummer, brought Lyric back from his fugue state. Lyric shook his head, remembered where he was and said, "Shit, lost my train of thought there. I must be getting old." He gave a wry smile, his teeth flashing under the bright lights as he counted off the intro to his next song. But he wasn't really feeling it after that; he was just going through the motions.

There was no note in his dressing room that night; it was under the windscreen wiper of his tour bus instead. The rose had been replaced by a book of Jim Morrison's poetry called, 'An American Prayer.' The inside had been gutted and shaped to hide a revolver. Lyric stood in the headlights of the revving bus wondering just where the hell that gun might be... and what exactly she planned on doing with it.

The note said, 'I got to keep moving, blues falling down like hail, blues falling down like hail. And the days keep reminding me, there's a Hellhound on my trail... Hellhound on my trail.'

Lyric boarded the already full bus, taking his usual place at the back and tried to drink himself to sleep. Just before Morpheus claimed him for his own, her face was in front of his, hissing and screeching in a bad approximation of his singing and her ragged tongue was licking his face. He awoke with a shout. It took a handful of Quaaludes to bring him down this time.

The next few weeks were a blizzard of songs, imagined wrongs, cheap whores and encores. His temper was getting the better of him. Constantly on edge and on the lookout for the girl (if that was indeed what she even was) in the audience, he began to understand the expression, "Sleep with one eye open." But even his dreams offered no respite from her. She was everywhere.

Time on the road is no time, Lyric once said. Each day bleeds into one. The food all begins to taste the same; so too, do the groupies. The drugs don't get you any higher and the whisky just tempers the spirit instead of making it soar. Each hotel room is identical to the one before, and some days you don't even know where you are. You have to rely on the promoter to tell you.

It was the only life Lyric knew, and despite the drudgery, he loved it, lived for it, it was who he was; and the songs he played night after night were his family; his constant companions on the road of life. Band members and roadies came and went but the songs remained the same.

Night after night, in every club and every city she was in the audience, and with each performance she came one step closer to the stage, her face growing bigger, like a waxing moon that reflected Lyric's worst fears upon him.

It was his love of the music that got him through—barely. The space between the notes was where Lyric squatted like a toad in the Bayou. Those tiny gaps were filled with endless possibilities for Lyric to monopolise on, to go one way or the other... up or down, left or right, heaven or hell. And when he played, the notes fell like snowflakes; no descent followed more than once, every song an original. It was in this sacred place that he could sometimes forget what was happening around him; it offered the flimsy illusion of sanctuary and was a blessed reprieve.

"So what do you wanna hear next?" growled Lyric, lighting a cigarette and taking a sip of his beer. They were at the revived Barnyard and the audience was going wild. Lyric had played there back in the late sixties supporting the Grateful Dead. Some wit near the back yelled, "Freebird!"

Lyric dragged his finger across his throat and pointed out into the darkness, then flipped the unseen voice the bird. Someone closer to the stage shouted, "Dust my Broom": an old blues standard recorded by Robert Johnson back in 1934.

"Dust my broom? Dust my Broom?" Lyric said, in a voice that was both high and incredulous. He looked down at his guitar, fiddled with some knobs, looked up and said, "Dust my Broom... shit man, how about, Suck My Cock?" Lyric laughed, and the people standing shoulder to sweating shoulder in the audience, laughed too.

He saw her again that night. He might have been the town drunk but he wasn't the village idiot. She was not a figment of his tired, toured out brain; nor was she a symptom of an undigested burger, a splash of mustard, several slices of Swiss cheese and a handful of underdone fries. There was definitely something more of the grave than of gravy about her.

You don't grow up in the Delta without seeing a few ghosts thought Lyric, and that's what she has to be. What else is there? Lyric knew that by the end of the tour she would be in the front row... looking up at him with those yellow eyes and jagged smile. What would happen after that was anyone's guess. Got to keep it together man, I can't afford to wig out, not now. I've worked too damn long and too damn hard to fuck this up.

His tour had followed the long arc of the sun heading relentlessly west aiming for L.A. Night after night she was there; dancing, gyrating lewdly to some rhythm other than what Lyric and his band were playing. And as quickly as she materialised she would be gone, disappearing like a spectre under the full weight of the noon day sun.

Then there were the gifts and cards which charted every sinister blues libretto ever penned. Lyric kept them all in a wooden cigar box that he stuffed into the bottom of his suitcase: a swatch of shiny jump-suit material, a beaded strand of flaming red hair, and a piece of the head-stock from a Fender Stratocaster had all been added to his collection.

It reached a head when she left a pair of bloody granny glasses on his motel pillow with the words,' Rape! Murder! It's just a shot away..." written on the back of a photograph of Lyric outside the Astoria, shaking hands and signing autographs. There were black crosshairs scratched over Lyric's face.

The following day they were in McCullum. Big club called the Persephone, with lots of blues fans and was guaranteed to be a great evening. Lyric knew someone who lived there, someone he prayed could help him—a talented singer and ex-lover, and their parting had been explosive rather than sweet sorrow. He hoped that time had healed those wounds, because he needed her help... badly, but if she didn't, he would understand completely.

What he had done to her was one of the many low points in his chequered past. She had fallen pregnant with his child and Lyric told her he didn't have enough love in his heart for two people, maybe not enough for even one. Or maybe he was just scared.

The woman Marie caught him in bed with a week later meant nothing at all to him; she was just Lyric's way of saying 'fuck off.' Hell, he didn't even know her name, but that didn't stop Marie from dragging the girl out of the bed by her hair and throwing her, naked, off the balcony.

Their relationship exploded in a shrieking crescendo of accusations and recriminations that drowned out even the wail of the sirens. The look in Marie's eyes as she was led away in handcuffs should have told Lyric just how badly he'd hurt her, but he was just too self-absorbed to notice or to care. She was just another groupie; a notch on his bedpost. That was what he told himself, but it was a lie and he knew it even then. It was Marie, and it always would be.

They crossed paths several times over the years, at the funerals of mutual friends, and they would nod at one another over the hole in the ground as the priest did his thing. He never asked about the baby. He didn't need to; the dead look in her eyes told it all, and he was never quite sure if it was relief or regret he saw reflected in them.

Lyric needed her now after all these years, not because of the love she once held for him, but because she had the gift and understood the worlds that lie just beneath the surface of our own. She journeyed between them, carrying messages from one side to the other. She practiced Voodoo, Hoodoo and a whole lot more, just like all the women in her family before her.

Lyric put a call through and begged her for all he was worth. She acquiesced finally, reluctantly, and arranged to meet him at a roadside diner called the 'Delphi' an hour out of the city.

Lyric parked his rental car and went inside the busy diner. He held the token-filled cigar box tight in his hand as he navigated a long room filled with feasting truck drivers. The air was blue with smoke that hung in layers like sheets of floating spider web. He was nervous.

Marie LaVeau sat alone smoking a cigarette, sipping demurely from a coffee cup. A half-eaten meal was pushed to one side. Marie had gotten her life back on track and left the rock 'n' roll lifestyle behind her, settling in a small town in the southern-most reaches of the lower 48; the kind of place that Lyric and his aching joints avoided like the plague. But things had changed for Marie after Katrina so she moved north to McCullum to live with her sister and to continue her practise.

"Long time Lyric, how you been?" she said politely, putting down the cup and extending her hand. Lyric hesitated before taking it.

She hasn't changed much, maybe a few lines around her eyes and mouth, but that's it. I wish I could say the same about myself... I bet I look like hammered shit. Man, why did I ever let this one get away?

"Because you're a fucking asshole Lyric, that's why," she said out loud, startling him. Their past filled the silence between them. *What am I feeling? Guilt? Is that it? I don't normally feel this way, but after what I did to her, I understand why.*

He took her smooth elegant hand in his rough calloused one and felt the slightest trickle of energy pass between them.

Marie's eyes were always the conduit for her inner voice, he thought, and right now they looked...pissed off. Her nails were a furious red against the white Formica tabletop.

She pulled deep on her cigarette, blew the smoke up towards the lights and said, "I can tell why you're here, Lyric. The stink of that bitch is all over you."

Lyric slid into the booth placing the box on the table. "Who is she?" he asked, his heart beating faster in his chest. Marie looked out the window at a row of mountains dipped in orange and banded brown and black by the setting sun, regretting agreeing to see him

"Not who, but what... she's called Calamity, Lyric. She's the tenth Muse."

"Tenth Muse, what the hell's that?"

"According to Greek mythology there are nine Muses, one for every discipline of the arts from poetry to painting. They are said to enthuse you to create the things you do, but Calamity is said to have come after, with the advent of the Blues... or maybe even a bit later, with rock 'n' roll."

She took another drag of her cigarette before continuing. "She has nothing in common with her sisters, Lyric. What she inspires is the dark stuff, all twisted and nasty and vile, in honour of her left-handed nature. She lives on the anarchy and the chaos that surrounds that type of music."

"So what's her deal, what does she want with me?"

"What do you think, honey?" she said, matter-of-factly, blowing smoke out of her nose.

"You can't go your whole life singing about death and sorrow and not hope to pick up some...bad karma. The blues is sex and death all wrapped in one, Lyric. It's pain, suffering, and misfortune, and that's what sustains her. It's what gets her high... keeps her alive. She feeds on the rebellion and that 'fuck-you' attitude. But it always comes at a cost for those that she has inspired, those she has set on the path to success."

"What do you mean?" he asked, upset.

Marie leaned forward and lowered her voice. Her sentences became clipped as the sun sank.

"Remember Altamont?" she asked.

"Sure, who doesn't?"

"Well, it wasn't just a Hells Angel that killed that poor boy, it was Calamity too. She demanded a sacrifice for that show, and for the bands playing there that day, and she got it. The 27 Club? That's all her too. Sure, it may look like drugs or drink or suicide, but let me tell you, she's always there at the end to collect from her coterie of performers."

"But what is she collecting? Surely if we're dead then..."

Marie cut him off. "You, Lyric. That's what sets her aside from the other muses. They feed on the final product of the artists creation, not her... she feeds on the artist. She gets some when they're young, she gets some when they're old, but in the end, she gets them all; just as long as they're famous. It's the price you pay for success, Lyric. And with your album at number one and all these nominations and sold out gigs you got on her radar, and that's definitely where you don't want to be. It ain't a devil down at the crossroads outside Clarksdale, Lyric. It's the mother-fucking Muse, Calamity."

Lyric sat back, mechanically lighting a cigarette, adding to the grey fug that filled the diner. He went to the counter, ordered himself a beer with a whisky back, finished it quickly then ordered another. He thought about doing a bump of cocaine in the bathroom stall but canned that idea when he saw a couple of state troopers coming in the front door to hit the head. He grabbed his sweating beer bottle and went back to Marie.

"Shit, so what do I do now?"

"There's not much you can do, Lyric... she's fucking with you too. By sending you all these little gifts," she said, pointing at the open cigar box. "She's fattening your fear for the feast. You know, some she takes quietly, others...not so much. Ronnie, Stevie, Buddy, she plucked them out of the air. Robert Johnson she poisoned. Jim and Janice by heroin; the list goes on, Lyric, and it pains me to say it, it really does...but it looks like you're on it."

"So what you're saying is that I'm fucked?"

Marie looked down at her coffee cup, swilling the oily liquid from side to side. "Lyric, you and I go back a long time, and I know you better than most. I also know you're a cold hearted son-of-a-bitch who has never done anything for anyone if it didn't benefit you."

"Now hold on," said Lyric. He knew he was morally bankrupt, he'd just never heard it said out loud before.

She raised her hand to silence him. She had to restrain herself from slapping him with it.

"That doesn't make you any better or any worse than the millions of other people walking around in their skin...it just makes you who you are and, sadly, who you are is going to get you killed. The fame and fortune, Lyric, it comes at a price," she said, with genuine sadness in her kohl-ringed eyes.

"So what are you suggesting? That I go home and commit suicide?"

"You know," she said, "That might not be a bad idea. You always were a bastard, Lyric, but at least you were my bastard." She stood to leave and then paused. "Can I ask you something, Lyric?" He looked up at her with the guilt of his past actions on his face. "What?" he said morosely.

"Do you have any regrets? About us, I mean?"

"We had some good times, Marie, but that's all they were." He'd repeated this mantra so many times over the years that it came instinctively to his lips. It was almost like one of his songs.

"You'll never change, and you're going to die screaming, you selfish prick." She blew him a kiss then turned and walked away leaving Lyric with his head in his hands.

They were in L.A., playing at the Coliseum on the last night of the tour. Lyric had last been there in '74, opening for Vanilla Fudge, Iron Butterfly and Led Zeppelin. He couldn't remember many of the details, so it must have been a good concert.

Now, nearly forty years later, he was here again. Sixteen people died on the last night of the Storm Warning tour, as Lyric played his entire repertoire of murder ballads; the characters in the songs were dropping like flies. Fuck it, thought Lyric, if I'm going to go out, I'm going to make my show a great one.

"This is 'In My Time of Dying', or for you blues scholars out there, 'Jesus Make Up my Dying Bed'," said Lyric. He swigged deeply from a nearly empty bottle of Jack Daniels. He was drunk off his ass but he didn't care anymore. His band, The Fates, a group of musical miscreants and ne'er do wells, were as tight as any band he could hope for; tight, but loose and they did the song proud. There was one more track to go on the set list and Lyric hadn't seen her yet. He couldn't believe it; he thought that tonight would have been the night. Maybe I'm wrong...hell, it ain't over till the dead man sings anyway, he thought.

They segued straight into the last song of the evening, the last song of the tour. It was called 'Fifteen Minutes' and was based on Warhol's thoughts on fame. When they finished, the applause was long and loud. Lyric took a bow and fled the stage much to the surprise of his band who was expecting him to hang around and soak up the ambience, but Lyric had other things on his mind.

Lyric checked his dressing room. Nothing. Just regular gifts like bottles of Jack, baggies of coke, and a bunch of real flowers. The tour bus was equally devoid of ghoulish trinkets from dead rock stars.

The after party went on long into the night at Lyric's desert hideaway. He spent the evening apologising to everyone for everything he had ever done. People thought it was the drugs talking, but they accepted his slurred confessions anyway. Then he spent the rest of the night sequestered in his bedroom on the phone, talking drunkenly to his manager about how he needed to change his ways and start giving back to society as a whole. He tried to contact Marie several times, to apologise for what he had done to her all those years ago; but it just rang.

He was put to bed sometime before dawn and slept like the dead with Calamity-free dreams.

Sunlight skinned Lyric's eyelids setting off a chain reaction deep within the recesses of his sleeping brain. He blinked, groaned, and felt himself surfacing slowly. A thin hawser of mucous ran from his cocaine-clogged nose all the way down his cheek to his pillow. He flicked his eyes open and groaned again, feeling the pressure of a world-class headache building in his temples. His stomach rolled lazily as he tasted last night's revelry in his mouth. It was foul.

He sat up slowly and surveyed the damage to his house. He felt naked, raw, like an oyster on the half shell. Thank god the tour was over he thought. Last night had been...cathartic. He didn't think he'd ever had an end of tour party quite like that one, one where he actually opened himself up to the possibility of being nice for once.

He swung his legs over the side of the bed and onto the floor with his heart hammering from such trivial movements. He coughed long and deep and opened the sliding doors to the patio to let some fresh air into the fetid house. He padded through the detritus to the kitchen in search of a glass of water and a handful of Aspirin. That's when he saw her sitting at his glass dining table, smoking one of his cigarettes.

"You're up at last," she said cheerily. "I'll let you in on a little secret though, Pigmeat: you snore like a fucking animal."

The thought of her watching him while he slept made his nausea rocket, and last night's festivities exploded on to his wooden floor.

"Sit down before you fall down," she said. "You're no good to me dead...well, not yet anyway."

The tenth Muse grinned, revealing row upon row of yellow teeth that rolled forward from her cavernous maw. Lyric felt his bladder go and, like the proverbial lemon in the song, the juice ran down his leg.

"Oh, poor baby's pissed himself," she said, now standing and circling slowly toward him. She came to rest an inch or so from his terrified face. She was wearing a pair of ripped and faded denims, tie-dyed in what appeared to be blood, vomit, and other unmentionable stains. She had on a faded 'Rolling Stones' T-shirt, now more grey than the black it once was. On her forearm was a tattoo of a skull and a heart and the words, "Rock 'n' Roll will never die."

Lyric smelt her breath wafting over his face. It reeked of fish guts rotting in the sun, flyblown, boiling with maggots. He retched explosively. She gave him that cutthroat smile again as he wiped his mouth with the back of his trembling hand.

Lyric sat down heavily on a wicker chair cupping his privates, afraid of what she might do with those teeth of hers. Calamity seemed to read his mind and made snapping motions with her distended jaw while mimicking oral sex.

"Chomp, chomp, Lyric... I bet that's one party favour you'll never forget," she said, winking salaciously. There was a dribble of yellow foam at the cracked corners of her mouth.

"It's time to pay the piper, Lyric. You're famous now and ripe for the eating; last night was your swan song, baby." Lyric began to blubber like a small child, protesting, begging for a second chance.

"Now, now, now, Lyric... pull yourself together. What does Neil teach us? That it's better to burn out than fade away? Bob said that death isn't the end, and he's right, you know, your work will live on forever, it will be legendary," she said softly, her hair writhing around her underbelly face.

"And do you know what else is going to be legendary, Lyric?" she asked, smirking, stroking his cheek.

"No...what?" he replied, not really wanting to know.

"Your pain," she shrieked, and fell on him.

It was over in mere minutes. Lyric lay on his back staring up at the ceiling thinking of all the bad he had done in his life. His vision began to swim as he felt the cold, clammy hands of death on his naked, bleeding body. He watched Calamity rocking back and forth on her heels, a huge bloody smile plastered on her gaunt face. The smell of his blood was in what was left of his nose. He began to cough. He swore he could hear hell's bells calling him home; and that's when he saw her, staring down at him. Marie. Or was it Calamity? Oh my god, it was Marie. She looked calm and at peace with what she had done. Their faces flitted back and forth until he could no longer distinguish who was what anymore. She squatted down on her haunches and whispered savagely in his ear. He knew then that it wasn't his fame that had brought him low, it was gifts squandered and opportunities wasted. It was a lifetime of regret and dirty deeds that could never be undone. And in the end it was Marie. Always Marie.

THE PALM READER
MATTHEW BOTTIGLIERI

"Shall we begin?" Issachar flipped the client's hand. "I can tell that you're nervous. That's nothing to be ashamed of; the future can be a frightening thing to face." Smiling, Issachar dragged his fingers the length of a pair of lines that stretched across the middle of the man's palm. "Your heart line and head line intersect. This informs me that your head and heart often conflict with one another."

"I don't need to read your palm to surmise that your heart probably wins most of those conflicts. We don't begin listening to our heads until our temples are gray, when it becomes too tiresome to fulfill the demands of our heart. Many people, unfortunately, are betrayed by their hearts, long before they have a chance to hear what their mind has to tell them."

Issachar sipped some wine. "Am I making sense?"

The client, a young man with dark hair, nodded.

Issachar cast his shadow across the man's palm and continued to scrutinize the lines. He clicked his tongue as he charted the routes engraved in the flesh like cartography. He didn't stop until a draft slipped under the door and gooseflesh erupted across his forearms.

"Are you cold?" Issachar draped a fur-lined cloak across his shoulders.

The man shook his head.

"You're being polite, my taciturn friend. I've been so engrossed in charting your palm that my courtesy has died along with the fire." Issachar rang a bell and a eunuch attended to the fire. "I had no idea that I was going to entertain a guest this evening; please excuse my rudeness."

When the eunuch departed, Issachar returned his attention to the man's palm. "Where were we?" He twisted his mouth. "Ah! I remember now. Everyone one is eager to know about their life line. The life line is less important than we think. We are all going to die—most of us anyway. The line that really matters is one's fate line. Our fate determines what befalls us." Gold teeth gleamed in the candle light. "I'll get to your fate in a little while. I have some other things to tell you, first."

Issachar measured the length and width of the man's palm and consulted a chart written in pig's blood on a sallow strip of papyrus. He inspected the thumb, from the tip to the base. When he finished with the thumb, he folded his hands behind his head and stared at the ceiling. "How shall I put this? Palmistry isn't concerned with one particular line."

He stood and leaned on his table and stretched his short legs. "To be sure, each line can be interpreted individually, but that is not what we're getting at. Life is infinitely more tangled and complicated than the lines creasing this palm of yours. I like to think that these lines work together. One must consider the entire map while one scrutinizes each line to develop a comprehensive sense of the person."

Issachar paced about the octagonal room and stared at the bookshelves that were crammed with dusty books, scrolls, rare stones, and bones. He stopped to scratch a grey cat between the ears before he returned to his seat. When he sat down again, he said, "Now, after reviewing the shape of your thumb, I am sorry to tell you that I detect deficiencies in your capacity for logical thinking and willpower." Issachar pointed to the middle segment of the thumb. "Yes, it is clear as day: your thumb's shape and creases reveal a lack of circumspection on your part."

The man's brow furrowed in confusion.

"Forgive me," said Issachar. "A lack of circumspection means that you're not careful." He tugged his thick black beard. "It seems that your proclivity for following your heart has less to do with immaturity and more to do with an inability to think clearly."

The palmist fed a handful of figs into his mouth. "Perhaps you've spent too much time in your cups, or you've lounged around in one opium parlor too many." Issachar shrugged. "Perhaps you were born mentally deficient. Whatever the case, I hope that you take as much time as you require from now on, to ponder the consequences of your actions—a difficult proposition for a young man with limited faculties and a proclivity for thinking with his heart instead of his head."

Sweat slithered down the bridge of the man's nose.

Issachar said, "Now, to countervail this bad news, take a look at the robust line on the opposite side of your palm. It reassures me a little bit. The line indicates that you're a vigorous young man. Your vigor enables you to withstand whatever life throws at you—whether sickness, stupidity, or acts of God." Issachar patted the hand. "You see? I told you that the lines have a way of accommodating one another. The good cancels out the bad, and vice versa."

After another mug of wine, and some more figs, Issachar inspected the rest of the man's fingers. He dragged his long nails across whorls of flesh. He hovered over a callous here and a scar there. He employed a magnifying glass to determine where one crease began and another ended. He measured and referred to more charts. He felt the man watch him, but it didn't unsettle him. He was used to scrutiny.

After he finished, Issachar scratched the top of his head. "I won't bore you interpreting the rest of your fingers. These measurements are too abstruse to explain. Suffice it to say they reveal information about the previous lives that one has lived. These considerations are beyond our purview, however, so forgive me for digressing."

Issachar clapped his hands together and studied the young man's life line. "Very nice," he said. "See how your lifeline curls like the tail of a cat around the ball of your thumb? You will likely live a long life. You will endure unspeakable hardship, but your blessed vitality and your untarnished life line indicate that you will survive it."

The young man said nothing.

Issachar dragged a fingernail down the man's fate, which stretched the entire length of his palm. "Your fate line, unfortunately, is jagged—crooked, even." He leaned on his elbows. "It is bisected by creases and scars. This is inauspicious. This is awful—tragic, to be honest. The jagged contours of your fate suggest that your long life will be marred by tragedy and suffering." Issachar scratched his beard. "Indeed, I can see that you are no stranger to tragedy."

"Your presence in my home this evening confirms that you have been the architect of many of these tragedies. I do not doubt, however, that some of these tragedies were beyond your control. You are of course not responsible for the fact that some whore shit you from her womb and left you to rot in one of the slums across the river." Issachar studied the fate line further. "It can't have been easy living hand-to-mouth, begging, stealing, and peddling your ass for a few shekels or a crust of bread." Issachar emptied his cup and filled it again. "It might have been kinder to drown you at youth to spare you the misery that life imposed upon you. These injustices probably would've killed a less vigorous boy, but you survived, like a roach."

Issachar wiped sweat from his forehead and picked up the cat and placed him on his lap. "A vigorous, athletic boy like you must have succeeded quite well at picking pockets and mugging. You probably know the ins and outs of the city's cesspits like the back of your hand—or your palm, as it were." Issachar laughed. "Forgive me, dear boy. My jokes are almost as bad as my manners." Issachar fixed his eyes upon the young man. "I think your troubles began when you peered across our city's filthy river at the stately homes and you coveted what was inside them." Issachar cleared his throat. "Don't misunderstand me, boy. I don't like my neighbors, either, and I wish that you'd chosen one of their homes to burgle instead of mine."

He tapped the man's palm. "But, as the lines in your palm instruct us, fate is often cruel." Darkness knitted Issachar's face. "You should've stayed with the rest of the trash on the other side of the river." He paused for a few moments and let the gravity of his words sink in. "If you'd escaped, it wouldn't have hurt me in the slightest to replace what you'd stolen." He tapped his fingers on the table. "I am going to give you something far more valu-able than the trifles that you attempted to steal from my home. I plan to spend the rest of your life teaching you the meaning of the words circumspection and consequence."

Flames sprouted from Issachar's eyes and scattered the shadows in the room. "You probably never dreamed that a necromancer lived in one of these pretty homes."

The young man's eyes dilated with terror and a moan rattled from his throat.

"When I am through with you, boy, you will feel, rather than know, the meaning of circumspection and consequence. I'll sear their meaning into the marrow in your bones."

Issachar watched the young man, shackled to a stone column at the opposite end of the room, cry and struggle against his chains. He reached down, picked up the man's severed hand from the blood soaked table and fed it to the hungry flames. A shriek spewed from the man's mouth.

As the man's shrieks filled the chamber, Issachar sifted through the knives, saws, picks, and plyers that were also strewn across the table. "It is unfortunate that I removed your tongue already. I too sometimes lack circumspection. Consequently, I'll never hear your side of the story, nor will

I ever learn your name." He stared at the young man a bit longer and watched him struggle against his shackles. He laughed at the trail of urine that spilled down the man's leg.

When the boy quit struggling and dangled from his chains, exhausted, Issachar said, "Well, your right hand told me a great deal about you." He picked up a rusted saw. "Let's see what your left hand has to say."

WORMHOLES
MARY QUIJANO

I wake up and instantly know that the world has changed in some subtle, indefinable way.

An earthquake rumbles under my bed, my heart accelerates for a moment and the sky momentarily darkens. Or am I still asleep?

I stumble to my computer and check the USGS website for my area: Nothing. Nothing!? Maybe a delay in reporting it...Or am I simply dreaming?

I grope my way back to bed, instantly drifting off into the comforting blackness, losing myself in the dream of waking and checking the computer. Earth rumbles again and then is still. I hardly notice.

After a time I get up and stagger to the bathroom, taking a piss without bothering to turn on the light. I shower, hot as I can stand it until the heat begins to run out, then grab a towel and rub it all over my slightly hairy, slightly scrawny body, rough enough to wake me up. Okay, I'm good.

A quick glance in the mirror convinces me that I'm still here, still who I thought I was when I went to bed last night. But that's about the last thing I'm going to find today that's normal.

I throw on an old sweatshirt that passes the sniff test, jeans that do not, and head to the corner for a paper cup of coffee and the morning newspaper, determined to show that bitch at the unemployment office that I am not some deadbeat leaching off the good citizens of this country, but someone actually looking for work.

The newsstand guy is strangely quiet today, as are the rest of the people milling about on the street looking for something they lost or somewhere to go. Everyone seems a little out of it, as if they forgot where they parked. The air seems different as well, a city of three million souls holding its collective breath and tiptoe'ing about its daily chores; and the whole thing starts to make me a little nervous.

I grab a hot dog from the vendor's cart, after a momentary debate on whether or not it's the best breakfast choice; have him add a splotch of sauerkraut for good measure, in utter defiance of the silent mother on my left shoulder, and hurry back to my apartment.

As I scratch the key into the rusty lock, my nearest neighbor, Mrs. Alvarez, exits her own pad shoving her recalcitrant adolescent son Tito ahead of her.

"Hey Mrs. A, hey Tito; off to school?" I call out cheerily, just to piss off Tito. He greets me with an upcurled lip and middle finger, a love greeting between buds. Mrs. A slaps his hand, shrugs at me with an apologetic little "what can you do" grimace, and walks back inside without a word, slamming the door behind her.

Tito, I notice, carries neither books nor backpack, and I wonder just how close he'll get to Franklin Delano Roosevelt High School today: Probably about as close as yesterday.

I consume the hot dog in two gulps, wash the sticky lump down with some scalding bitter coffee, and turn to the classifieds, circling any help wanted postings that I might even remotely qualify for.

I try calling a few, but today the static on my cell phone is even worse than usual, and after three or four dropped calls I decide to call it a day and lay down for my midday nap.

When I get up a couple of hours later I am immediately hit by a wall of absolute silence, though it takes me a minute to realize what is wrong: There is none of the usual racket from outside. Everything is dead quiet.

The world has shifted.

What is the scariest thing you can imagine?

For me, I discover, it's to wake up, and not be where you were, to not be anywhere: To find that the world has disappeared, everyone and everything in it but you, because you were left behind, unworthy. The rapture or whatever has happened, and you were left behind and there is nothing remaining but you in this little dreadful apartment in the middle of a city that no longer exists in a country that no longer exists on a planet that no longer exists.

I look out the window and there is nothing there. No skyscrapers, no bums, no neon lights, no angry honking traffic, no gang-bangers swaggering home from a night of drugs and pussy, no dirty streets or noisy trash trucks or buses or taxis or cops or hookers. NOTHING.

Outside my window there is not even an opaque grey mist, neither light, nor dark: just an endless expanse of nothing at all that goes on and on forever. My heart takes an adrenalin leap, bashing into my chest at mach 5 until I feel faint and sick. That frantic beating I can hear, that much is still real. But where am I?

Is this Nirvana? Did my endless attempts at meditation while on Salvia or some more lasting, more potent mind altering concoction finally put me in that place I seek? Or am I locked into some druggy high, OD'd on some chemical never to return again?

But I didn't take anything, not last night, not this morning. Not for weeks, other than a little too much cheap beer. And I can't be dead, can I? I'm too young, too healthy.

Wait a minute: did everything else go, or did I go? Does the world I once knew still exist somewhere, but I'm no longer in it? Was I simply plucked like a bug off a leaf, put in some glass bottle to be scrutinized by some unknown, unseen gi-normous being who is liable to get bored at any moment and drop me into a specimen jar full of isopropyl alcohol, no time for even a quick drunken high before it sucks the life out of me, leaving my well-preserved little human form—slightly hairy, slightly scrawny—to stare sightlessly out at an endless queue of alien high school students taking note of my structures in their version of Bio 101.

"What the hell, where is everyone!!"

I scream it out the window, but my voice is absorbed into the empty void and swallowed without a sound

I slam the window closed, suddenly afraid that emptiness will pervade every part of my room until it finds me. I sit down on the couch, moving my butt around until I locate the sweet spot where the springs don't poke me. What the fuck, what the fuck, what the fuck, I mutter over and over, shaking my head.

I grab my cell phone and dial Leslie. He'll know what to do. But, of course, there's no dial tone, no cell phone tower, no call to go through, and no one to receive it. I turn on the TV, but it doesn't. Just sits there, dead. Okay, okay, what do I do? I've got a little food in the 'fridge, a few cans of tuna, tomato soup and refried beans in the cupboard. Not much, but maybe enough for a few days if I'm careful.

I wonder if the rest of the building is still here: I'm on the third floor of this dilapidated ghetto walk up, so maybe there's someone left in the building besides me.

I take a deep breath, then yank open the front door of my apartment: sure enough, the hallway outside still exists, torn urine-stained carpet, graffitied walls and all. I feel strangely comforted by this shabby reminder of the world

I live in.

"Hello?" I call. "Anyone there? Mrs. Alvarez? Tito? Anyone?"

No one responds. After a minute, I creep down the hallway, keeping close to the gang-deco wall, and carefully avoiding those spots where I know the wood floor under the filthy carpet will creak. I get to the next apartment and try to look through the little magnifier peep-hole in the door, but it's too smeared with years of accumulated dust and air grime to let me see anything, even after I wipe off my side of the lens with the tail of my shirt. I bang on the door, but not too loud...I don't want anyone else to hear me besides the Alvarez family.

No one answers. I call out again: "Mrs. Alvarez? Tito?"

Silence greets me. I try the door, and it isn't locked, so like Goldilocks I figure what the hell, unlocked means come on in, right?

Their apartment, it turns out, is a clone of mine...only about twice as cluttered and dirty, as if that's possible. Poor lady works all night cleaning office buildings and then comes home to this: I oughta put Tito up against a wall somewhere, if I can still find one intact. I skulk from room to room, which is to say from the filthy kitchen with its piles of unwashed dishes, pizza boxes and fast food wrappers to the even filthier bathroom in which remnants of every gross human byproduct is still in evidence; and thence to the two small bedrooms. I look for bodies under the piles of unwashed clothes on the floor, the tumble of blankets on the beds, but find no remains. Suddenly I feel something brush up against my leg and I scream like a six year old girl.

It's their cat Conchita, probably the only pretty and well-cared for thing in the house...if not in the entire building. She's a fluffy grey Persian which I'm pretty sure Tito lifted from some pet store as a Mother's Day present two years ago. Mrs. Alvarez knew better than to ask questions, just laid out her string of "gracias" and "que bueno"s, replete with hands clasped to oversized bosom and multiple wet kisses on the pimply cheeks of her youngest son, for whom she still held out great hopes. I think the rest of the brood are already doing time somewhere, but Tito has managed to stay under the radar and out of gangs for most of his 17 years, which is a new record in this neighborhood.

I scoop up the oversized cat in my arms and hold her to my face, happy to have found anything alive to talk to. Unfortunately it takes only about 13 seconds for my allergies to kick in, and I have to put her down until I stop a violent bout of sneezing.

"So where's your Mama and Uncle Tito?" I ask the cat finally.

No answer.

"Gone away, you say? You think they'll be back soon? No? Well, surely they won't mind if I help myself to whatever food they might have left behind for us, right?"

Chi Chi, which is what Tito calls her when Mama Alvarez isn't within earshot, lets out a soft bleat, and that's good enough for me. I find an unopened jar of peanut butter, a half a loaf of bread and some Oreos on the counter, and a small bag of cat food in the cupboard, which is about all I can manage to carry in one arm while holding the cat in the other.

Back in my room, after I put away the borrowed groceries, Chi Chi and I stare at the walls. She doesn't seem quite herself either, although in all honesty I haven't ever spent enough time around cats to know what's normal or not. But for a cat to just sit there staring, as if she sees something I don't, that bothers me. Especially when she lets out those low little growls, just under her breath, like maybe she's afraid to be heard by whatever it is that's making her nervous.

I try the TV again—vain hope—and then my cell phone. Still nothing. No lights work either, and the refrigerator is warming up in the September heat. I decide I'd better eat what's in there before it rots, so I start with the chocolate fudge brownie ice cream as that's the first likely to go.

Somehow all that fudgy deliciousness makes me feel better, at least for the moment.

I look around for something to read, but all I brought with me when I moved this last time was my favorite China Mieville novel that I've already read twice, and the entire Dark Tower series. I could read that again, I suppose, but it seems like a poor choice considering the present situation. Besides, if I'm stuck in here long enough to finish it, I'll be dead well before they get to the tower. Then there's that box in the corner, wrapped in plastic and duct taped in multiple layers. That one contains reading material I'd love to get into: my life's collection of comic books. But they're still in the original wrappers, mint condition, and I'd die before I'd unwrap a single one.

I pick up The Gunslinger by default, browse through a few pages then put it down and walk over to the window. Cautiously I draw back a tiny flap from the bottom corner to peek outside, hoping that the drug induced hypnosis is finally over and I can check myself into the psych ward of the nearest hospital to drain all remnants out of my system and check for damages. But the emptiness beyond remains, a vast, silent void. I drop the curtain edge and back quickly away, returning to my seat on the couch, my hands between my knees like a kid in the principal's office waiting verdict.

What the hell is going on? What's happened to the world?

I open my door a crack and look out into the hallway, then a step further and look to the left as well. The apartment building still seems normal from here, other than the absence of life or sound. It's like it's waiting for something, like the world beyond its walls has taken a deep breath, held it, and is waiting to exhale.

I go back inside and sit there, tapping my fingers on my knees.

"What you think, Chi Chi? Think anyone else is in the building, maybe knows what's going on?"

The cat looks up at the sound of my voice, then goes back to grooming herself. Priorities.

"I'm going to leave you for a little while, okay kitty? Don't go anywhere, promise?"

I slip out my apartment door, closing it silently behind me. It's a small apartment building, just four apartments on each of the three floors, two on either side of the central stairwell. I try Mrs. Alvarez again first, but I left her door cracked open and nothing's changed, so I go to the two flats on the left instead, knocking softly on the doors and calling to whoever might be inside No answer, either time; and both doors are locked, although I think I hear something growling quietly in Apartment 3d that sends a chill down my back and into my groin.

I hurry back towards my apartment, ready to flee inside, then get a grip on myself.

"Check downstairs, idiot," I say aloud.

On the second floor, the situation is the same: no one home; at least none who will answer my knock or my call, and all doors locked. I glance down the broad stairway towards the ground level entrance, wondering if I should check the apartments there, too. But beyond the glass door of the entrance lies that emptiness: I see it even though it isn't there; it hangs outside the safety of this last little remaining piece of the world like an invisible abyss, waiting for me to slip.

I run up the stairs and back into my room, slamming and locking the door behind me, then sit down on the sofa again, shaking. Chi Chi appears from under the sofa and crawls into my lap, as if wanting comfort, but when I start to stroke her fur she suddenly hisses and strikes out with her claw, scratching my arm, then runs away to hide beneath the bed.

"Whatever," I say, frowning and rubbing my arm. "Stupid cat; when I run out of food just watch your back."

I'm not hungry, but I open and eat a can of tuna with some crackers and wonder what time it is.

Neither clock nor cell phone nor computer nor TV can answer that question, and there is no sense of day or night beyond these walls to give a hint of time either. It's all one big present time moment, the endless now.

Once again I wonder if perhaps I've reached Nirvana, that tantalizing goal of all mystics. If I did, I need to go back and tell them it's actually pretty boring. I'd like to sleep, but I'm afraid that if I do I might wake up to find everything gone, including myself. I shake my head, knowing that doesn't make sense; but what does any more?

I'm just starting to doze off despite myself, when there is a faint rap at the door. I'm not even sure it's real, until I hear it again, accompanied by a faint desperate plea: "Let me in, damn it!"

"Who is it?" I call through the door.

"What the hell does it matter? Let me in!"

I can't really argue with that logic, so I crack open the door an inch, and it is immediately flung aside by a girl in her early twenties wearing four inch stacked heels, runny mascara, a tiny pair of shorts and a top more suited to Victoria Secret lingerie ads than street wear.

"Whoa!" I say.

"Yeah, I'm a hooker, so...got anything to eat? And by the way, don't even think about sex."

"Right. Well, okay; I've got some tuna and frankly, under the circumstances, I very much doubt I could get it up, so no worries."

I give her a can of my tuna and a handful of crackers, and just watch her eat for a while, happy enough with that.

"My name's Candy," she tells me when she notices me staring, spewing cracker crumbs.

"Really," I say.

"Okay, well actually it's Sheila. I'm from Dayton; or I was five years ago. Got anything to drink?"

I sigh as I get up to find her a warm diet coke. I don't really want to hear her life story, or how she came out here hoping to become a starlet. I figure if you decide all you got to exchange in the open market is what's between your legs, then maybe you just didn't try hard enough, but that's not for me to say. Anyway, it's the end of the world as far as I can tell, so it's a little late for recriminations.

"So, what brought you to L.A.?" I ask, deciding to let her tell her story if it makes her feel better: It's the least I can do.

"When I hit fourteen my stepdad suddenly found me...attractive," she says, looking down. "He found me like that for about a year, until my mom discovered what was going on. She bought me a one way ticket to L.A., said don't come back." Her voice catches on this last, and I see a solitary tear drop onto her lap.

"So you became a hooker?"

I probably could have said that in a little gentler way, but time was short.

She shrugs. "You grow up thinking things are going to be fair, but fair just means everything goes the way you want it to, and that never happens, does it?"

"Pretty much, no," I say. "I think you write the story of your own life, and survive by default."

"Oh yeah?" she says, wiping her nose. "Then who's writing this?" She waves her arm towards the nothingness outside our windows.

I'm thinking how to answer when the room starts shaking.

"Oh crap, oh crap," she says, grabbing hold of me. We stand there in the middle of the room, wild eyed and panting until the tremor stops.

"What's going on, Jacob?" she cries. "Why is this happening? I don't understand."

I have nothing I can tell her, no science, no philosophy, no religion to explain the disappearance of our world.

"I thought maybe I'd died," I tell her; "that maybe this was like limbo or hell or purgatory...I knew it wasn't heaven 'cause I never was good enough for that."

"Me neither," she admits. "But when I heard you in the hallway calling out, I thought: 'No, that sounds too normal, too human to be like a near death experience."

"Were you awake when it started, whatever this is?"

"Kinda; well, not really. My last John stayed the night and wanted more and more, you know. So I kept givin' him what he wanted until he ran out of funds, then I sent him packing and tried to get some sleep. I was just drifting off when I felt something weird, like a wave of energy pass through the room. Made me feel a little dizzy, a little sick to my stomach, like when you're out on a boat, you know?"

"Motion sickness," I nodded. I was actually beginning to feel a bit queasy myself now.

56

"Right after that, everything went real quiet. I like to sleep with the TV on to drown out all the other noise, but when that went off it was like everything else did too. I got scared and started to run outside, thinking maybe there was another 9-11 or something, but that's when I saw it all disappear."

"What do you mean, what did you see?" I demand.

"I, I just saw it fade, starting with the buildings in the distance, then closer and closer. First they would start to stretch, then they would get fainter and fainter, and then they were gone. I ran back upstairs and slammed my door and crawled under my bed and waited to disappear too. When I didn't, I just stayed there, curled up into a little ball, waiting for I don't know what. I think I fell asleep for a while: Then I heard you."

"Shit," I say. "I have no fucking idea what is going on."

"You wanta have sex?" She says, but I know she's only scared and trying to be nice, not knowing any other way to express it.

"Thanks, but I seriously can't get it up right now," I say, then give her a hug so she won't feel like I don't like her or something.

"Okay."

We sit there, staring at each other. Chi Chi comes out from under the sofa and stares at us as well. Then the building begins to tremble again, and this time it doesn't stop.

Sheila reaches out and takes my hands, as the walls of the apartment slowly fade, stringing out into the void, first the walls, the windows, the curtains. The TV starts to go, the chair and the desk. I cry out as my double-secure-taped box of first edition mint condition comic books leaves us for some other dimension.

Conchita is next: letting out a squeal and a hiss, she is all eyes and claws and hair on end as she is pulled out like a length of taffy fading into the ether. I hold onto Sheila as long as I can; her desperate expression the last thing I see before she disappears, and then it is my turn.

I feel an incredible force pulling at me, and as I give in and let go, I become suddenly aware that this black hole is actually a living thing. Drawn closer, I see an enormous maw lined with row after row of tooth-like projections, grinding and grinding and grinding. My scream is swallowed by that yawning cavern of mouth into which the world and everything in it is rushing, dissolving back into the glowing essence of matter and energy from which it was created: I realize as my doom comes rushing up to find me that this world eater is, in form and function much like an immense earthworm, and we are simply a meal being sucked down into its gullet, with only the indigestible parts to be shat out the other end into a different dimension. But that won't include Sheila or Conchita, and it won't include me.

THE DANCERS ON THE WALL

ALEX J. CHRISTY

The crew of Yesterday knew the history and reputation of Rhomnus well—its glorious rise and mysterious fall, the subsequent years of neglect and abandonment, and the dark rumors that clung to it like a foul stench. So when they ran aground on a sandbar beneath that ancient city's moonlit ruins, more than a few cursed the gods for their ill luck. So eager was the crew to get clear of the ill-rumored ruins that they set to work with furtive haste, pushing and pulling with oars and long, hooked poles, working up a sweat despite the chill in the late autumn air.

After an hour, their labors were cut short by a cry from the lookout. The man pointed and all eyes turned in the direction of his quivering finger. There atop the moonlit walls of Rhomnus were the forms of people, garbed in crimson and dancing grotesquely. Not a sound accompanied their bizarre gyrations except for the hollow moan of the wind through the trees. Several sailors murmured dark oaths while others quaked or averted their eyes from the macabre display.

"Keep your heads, lads," said their captain, a tall, hook-nosed man named Fortwaith. "Those phantoms cannot harm us from up there, and the sooner Yesterday is free, the sooner we can leave this place behind." Encouraged by his words the crew mustered their grit and pressed on.

The red-garbed forms danced in silence throughout the night as the wary sailors labored on the ship below. Strangely, the captain showed little disquiet in their presence. He watched them with keen interest until the first grey hints of dawn shone in the eastern sky. As the sun cracked the horizon the dancers left, disappearing from the wall as silently as they had appeared.

Later that day the crew managed to pull the ship free, straining at the oars of their boats with many a nervous glance back at the now deserted walls.

Once the ship was in open water they clambered back aboard to await their orders. Captain Fortwaith stood silently upon the quarterdeck, his eyes focused on the ruins across the river.

The first mate, a young man named Tor Sheklas, stepped up to the captain. "Your orders, sir?" he asked quietly.

The captain glanced at Tor and blinked. "Raise anchor and resume our previous course," he said. "We head north." Tor nodded and called out to the rest of the crew as Fortwaith turned back to the walls of Rhomnus, a puzzled expression on his angular face. His gaze lingered on those strange ruins until long after they were lost from sight.

That night Fortwaith was vexed by lucid dreams of a bizarre and unusual nature. In his dreams he left his cabin and the ship, and flew south along the Grel River only a few meters above the turbulent waters. Cool wind whipped his hair and night robe behind him. Soon he spotted the moonlit walls of Rhomnus, upon which the crimson figures danced. He landed atop the wall and joined those strange dancers— men and women whose faces were hidden by dark veils, and whose hands and bodies gestured seductively beneath damp, red cloth. As he joined in their midnight celebrations something pulled at him. An inexorable force drew him away from the revelry and down towards the ancient city. He left the dancers and floated from the crumbling walls, gliding through abandoned streets lined with magnificent, ruined houses and the ghost-white skeletons of marble temples. Eventually he arrived at a still lake, from the center of which rose a dome-shaped island, greyish-green and slick with moss. As he surveyed the strange vista a small object caught his eye, half-buried in the dark sand near his feet. Thinking it merely a rock he ignored it at first, but then the clouds shifted and moonlight fell upon the object. It glimmered with a dull, metallic sheen. Fortwaith knelt down and dug the item out of the sand. It was a gold statuette, almost unrecognizable beneath layers of clinging silt. He brought it to the edge of the lake and rinsed it, the water clouding as he ran his thumbs over its pocked and pitted surface. As he crouched in the muddy shallows he spied similar objects strewn across the lakebed, partly buried in the black sediment and golden in the moonlight. There were hundreds of them at least, glittering in the muck. He raised the newly cleaned statuette before his eyes and gasped, falling back in awe. A wild thrill bubbled in his veins and he turned his eyes from the metal object to the dome-shaped island at the lake's center. With a sudden jolt Fortwaith awoke in his own bed, drenched in sweat, his heart pounding uncontrollably. He could recall nothing of what he saw in those last revelatory moments of his dream.

Fortwaith was haunted by the same dream every night for the next week, and it always ended as he uncovered the golden object and looked upon the island. As the days went by he ate little and slept less. What sleep he did manage was restless and filled with the same feverish imagery. His face grew drawn and haggard, and he kept mostly to his cabin. Occasionally at night he would emerge as if in a trance and stand silently upon the quarterdeck, his body swaying with the motion of the boat and his eyes focused to the south. The crew began to avoid him. They turned instead to First Mate Tor for guidance. Tor did not relish the situation but made the most of it, guiding the ship expertly northward.

On the tenth day of travel the ship made its destination, setting anchor in the clear, icy waters of Lake Maelfeurd near the barbarian town of Teurn. Upon arrival, a party of brawny Northmen pushed off from the stony beach to meet with the galley. Their longboats were laden with trade goods—pelts, ivory, precious amber and rare wood. As the barbarians neared Yesterday they lifted their palms in greeting, but when they spied the ship's gaunt captain standing crookedly upon the stern they stopped rowing. Their boats drifted to a halt several meters from the anchored galley. They stared silently at Fortwaith, unreadable expressions on their long, bearded faces. Tor leaned over the rail, his reddish hair and beard blowing in the cold wind.

"What is it?" he called to them in their own tongue, being half barbarian himself. "Why do you stop?"

One of the greybeard elders lifted his index finger and traced a curious symbol in the air before him. He then nodded towards Captain Fortwaith. "Faerbane," he said. With that the Northmen turned their longboats around and began rowing away from the ship.

Tor looked over at the pale captain. The man swayed on the deck, seemingly unaware of the interaction that just took place. His glassy eyes were focused to the south and his mouth worked silently, repeating some whispered mantra. He turned and shuffled back to his cabin, shutting the door behind him.

A young swab named Lively hobbled up next to Tor, his wooden leg tapping against the deck of the ship. "Sir, what did the old barbarian mean by that? Fare—"

"Faerbane," said Tor. "It means 'disease of the soul'."

Lively looked confused.

"A fancy way of saying cursed," said Tor.

"Oh," said Lively, shifting his weight nervously. The two men stood on the deck of Yesterday and watched the Northmen row slowly back to shore.

Tor knocked lightly on the captain's door. There was no answer.

"Sir?" He knocked again, a bit louder. Muffled sounds came from within. Papers shuffled and something heavy closed with a whumph.

"Who is it?" The captain sounded annoyed.

"It's Tor, sir."

Nearly a minute of silence followed. Tor was just about to say something else when the captain finally replied. "Come in then."

Tor opened the door and winced as a miasma of stale air wafted out—a pungent cocktail of body sweat and old, musty papers. The room was uncomfortably hot and dim, the only light coming from three portholes that were covered with crimson drapery. Tor stepped into the red-lit room and looked around. All four walls were plastered with hastily scrawled papers depicting drawings, diagrams, notes and other written works of indecipherable purpose. The floor was similarly littered with crumpled, discarded papers. To his right was the captain's cot. The bedding was disheveled, the bed likely left unmade for some time. A great oak desk dominated the center of the room, its surface covered with yet more scattered papers.

Captain Fortwaith reclined behind the desk in a plush armchair. Rumpled, sweat-stained clothing clung to his narrow, unwashed frame. His beard was scraggly and unkempt, his eyes red-rimmed and nervous. A heavy, leather-bound book lay before him on the desk. He drummed his fingers against it and tilted his head as Tor approached, forcing a smile.

"How goes our trade with the savages?" His voice was thick and raspy.

Tor bristled at the slur, but buried his anger quickly. "They refuse to trade with us, sir."

"Why not?"

"They fear that we are cursed." Tor was going to say you, but thought better of it. "Word must have reached them of our encounter near Rhomnus."

At mention of that city the captain's eyes glazed over. "Of course. Barbarians are a superstitious lot, after all. They fear that which they do not understand." He stared silently at the book in front of him for several seconds.

"Sir?"

Fortwaith turned his gaze back to Tor and the fog cleared from his eyes. "There must be some among them for whom profit is a stronger driving force than fear."

"I'm afraid not, sir. The Northmen view curses the way we do disease. To them we are contagious. None will come close to us for fear of catching the Faerbane, as they call it. And if we attempt to approach them, they will attack. Our business here is done it seems."

Captain Fortwaith leaned back in his chair and blew out a long sigh. He frowned and rapped his knuckles against the desk, slowly scanning the papers before him with their scribbled notes and odd drawings. Tor noticed an unsettling gleam light the captain's eyes.

"If the barbarians refuse to deal with us, then we will find our fortunes elsewhere." He quickly scooped together the notes on his desk and looked at Tor, a gargoyle's grin on his face. "We will return to Rhomnus."

Tor shook his head at the absurdity of the idea. "Sir, you cannot be serious."

"Oh I am quite serious." He waved a handful of papers at Tor. "I have been researching Rhomnus quite extensively these last two weeks. I believe that much of the city's legendary wealth still lies behind its walls, a vast, golden treasure buried in the mud of a forgotten lake."

"How do you know this?" asked Tor.

Fortwaith's eyes shifted wildly around the room as if fearing an eavesdropper before finally settling again on Tor. "I had a vision showing me the way."

"A vision, sir?" Tor was worried. Ambition was one thing, but this sounded like madness.

"Yes, a vision. Numerous visions in fact, the same one each night. In them I return to Rhomnus. Once there I dance atop the wall with the crimson folk, who welcome me as a brother." Fortwaith sounded wistful, and Tor grew more uncomfortable. "After our revelry I am led to a lake with an island at its center. Beneath the surface of the lake are hundreds of golden statues, each one of unimaginable value. I reach for them, and— ." Fortwaith trailed off and his brow furrowed.

"Sir?" said Tor.

"That is all I remember. The path to the lake is clear to me, that is all that matters."

Tor shifted uneasily. "What of these crimson folk?" he said. "They don't care that you mean to steal their wealth?"

"It is unlikely they realize the true value of these objects. Otherwise they wouldn't be at the bottom of a lake. Of course, should they want some form of recompense arrangements can be made. We undoubtedly have something in our cargo hold that would stir their interest." The captain grinned. "Who knows, they may prove better trade partners than the barbarians."

"Or they could prove our doom," said Tor. His mouth was a thin, dark line beneath his tangled beard.

Captain Fortwaith laughed. "Don't tell me you share your brethren's superstitions"

"No sir, I do not. But we do not know who these people are, or what their intentions may be."

"Where is your spirit of adventure, Tor?" Fortwaith rocked forward in his seat. "We are on the verge of acquiring undreamt-of wealth. Don't you want to be there when we dredge a priceless, golden hoard from the silt of that forgotten lake?"

Tor shook his head. "It doesn't feel right, sir."

"Bah, that's your barbarian half talking. But if that's how you feel, you can stay with the ship." The captain gathered his papers and began pouring over them with hungry eyes. "Tell the men to weigh anchor," he said without looking up, "we leave immediately."

Tor stood there for a moment, unsure of what to do. He turned and walked towards the door, but something in his gut stopped him. He knew that the captain was making a poor decision.

"Sir," he said quietly, "I'm afraid I cannot pass your message along." He turned and faced Fortwaith.

The captain was aiming a loaded crossbow at Tor's chest. He sighed. "Then I'm afraid I must relieve you of your duties." He pulled on a woven cord and somewhere a bell rang. A few moments later a sailor named Branson entered the room, stopping short to take in the tense, red-lit scene before them.

"Branson, please escort Tor below decks and put him in chains. You're first mate now."

Branson glanced at Captain Fortwaith then at Tor, unsure of what to do. Tor was his friend, but he couldn't disobey a direct order. Sensing the other man's hesitation, Tor placed his hands behind his back and nodded. Branson stepped forward and took Tor by the elbow.

Captain Fortwaith set the crossbow down stared at the half barbarian with cool, condescending eyes. "You're a fool, Tor. You'll realize that soon enough." He nodded at Branson. "Once Tor is secure below decks, raise anchor. We head south for Rhomnus."

After five days of swift travel downriver they arrived once more in the grey waters off the ruined city. The ship set anchor and they waited for nightfall. Most of the crew spent the night in the stuffy heat below decks, huddled in groups and whispering their displeasure. Fortwaith remained above, his hands on the gunwale and his unblinking, bloodshot eyes fixed upon the city.

That night the moon shone brightly, and close to midnight the wildly dancing forms returned to the wall, clad in crimson and luminescent in the lunar glow. Fortwaith shouted madly and called for his crew, feeling again the inescapable pull from his dreams. He quickly assembled a landing party to go ashore, a group of twelve reluctant souls.

From the anchored galley Captain Fortwaith and his men were lowered in a dinghy and rowed by moonlight towards an ancient, mossy canal that emptied along the riverbank. They glided silently into the mouth of the waterway. Soon the night sky was obscured by a thick canopy of branches and leaves. The sounds of the forest, so loud on the other side of the river, were absent here—even the ever-present buzzing of mosquitoes was missing. The men scanned the dark woods nervously as Fortwaith steered the rowboat through the still waters towards the base of the wall, where a thick, iron gate rose up and blocked the entrance to an arched tunnel of worked stone. The boat slid to a quiet stop in the black waters beneath the colossal gate, scraping up against an ancient quay of moss-covered stone. Without further word Fortwaith tied the boat off and leapt onto the quay. His tall, narrow body squeezed between the rusted bars of the canal gate. One by one the landing party followed, taking with them the long, hooked poles used weeks earlier to free Yesterday from the sandbar. Fortwaith said they would need them to retrieve the treasure. Only the young swab Lively remained behind, watching as the last of the landing party disappeared into the black shadows beyond the gate. On these excursions it was his duty to watch the boat, since the gnarled club of wood below his left knee made him ill-suited for long treks. He could handle a sword well enough though, and his eyes and ears were sharp, both of which made him valuable despite his missing leg. Besides, watching the boat was a task he didn't much mind under normal circumstances, and minded even less tonight. He listened as the party's steps grew fainter and fainter, and then limped over to a large, weathered stone to sit and await their return.

A silent hour passed as Lively sat alone, chewing his lip and glancing nervously into the shadows around him. There truly was something unnatural about this place, and as he waited in the dark all the stories of Rhomnus seemed to come back to him. In its prime, bards wrote songs about the marvelous beauty of Rhomnus. The Northern Jewel, as it was called, was renowned for its mosaic-adorned walls, green terraced gardens, crystal clear canals, and its breathtaking skyline of towers, parapets and domes. Pilgrims flocked yearly to its gilded gates, making it a great melting pot—not only of the human races, but of Fae and stranger beings still. It was a shining beacon of civilization on a savage continent.

But as glorious as the tales were of the city at its apex, the tales of its fall were just the opposite. Fifty years ago dark rumors of a terrible calamity spread from the city, stoked by pilgrims who found the gates closed. The small villages that once flourished within the city's shadow were ghost towns—the farms gone to weed, the mills to decay. Even animals shunned the surrounding hills and forests, or at least the more wholesome types of beasts did. And as the city's unsettling reputation spread, fewer pilgrims came to see it. Soon even explorers and adventurers gave up, the potential rewards unworthy of the risk. For five decades the doors of Rhomnus were sealed to the outside world, its fate a mystery and its people forgotten. In dockside bars in every port, stories were told of the fall of Rhomnus—of ancient curses and human sacrifice, of dark magic and deals made with inhuman beings. One legend claimed that there was a lake at the center of Rhomnus that had no bottom, and somewhere in its depths slept a god. A god who was worshipped before men walked the continents, and who would rise again when the stars were right.

Lively had little idea what the last bit meant about stars being right, but for now he was thankful that a thick canopy of leaves and branches obscured the vast night sky above him. Then again these were just rumors, exaggerated stories meant to entertain. Who could say what really happened to this city. He tried his best to put the dark thoughts out of his mind, but found the task difficult. An oppressive silence closed around him like some watchful predator—circling, waiting for the right moment to strike. Several times he spun around, positive that some hidden menace loomed over his shoulder. He found nothing there but an aura of palpable dread.

Another hour came and went and the silence became too much for him. He made up his mind to whistle a quiet tune, something nostalgic to keep the fear at bay. Thinking for a few moments he soon snapped his fingers and pursed his lips. He drew air into his cheeks for the first note.

Somewhere in the distance, behind the rusted gate and beyond the black shadows, there echoed a piercing scream.

Lively's eyes widened and the whistle left his mouth in a burbling leak. The scream climbed to a fevered pitch, and then with a final plaintive cry, it ended. He rose up slowly from his seat, his legs weak and jittering. The wooden tip of his left leg tapped and scraped against the mossy stone floor. His blood felt like ice water as he stared into the darkness beyond the gate. Soon another wail followed the first, and then another. In a few seconds a terrible symphony of screams emanated from somewhere in the distant city. The shrieking was amplified by the tunnel and was shockingly distinct in the pervasive silence. Small hairs rose on Lively's neck and arms, and his cheeks grew numb from fear. Unable to move, he could only stand and stare into the darkness until the screams eventually went quiet. When the last strangled shriek disappeared and silence resumed, he became aware of a new sound—footsteps on stone, getting closer.

The footsteps grew louder and heavier, approaching from the shadows somewhere beyond the gate. Lively drew his cutlass from his belt, fear issuing from his every pore. Suddenly a tall form burst from the darkness and slammed against the gates, shaking loose decades of orange-red rust. Lively cried out and raised his sword, putting his arm defensively in front of his face. A brief, tense moment passed as he shielded his eyes, and then a voice called hoarsely to him—a familiar one.

"Help me."

Lively lowered his arm and squinted at the form. He breathed a deep sigh of relief—it was Captain Fortwaith. Lively hobbled towards the gate, but faltered on closer inspection of the man. Blood dripped from the captain's hair and clothing in syrupy strands. His eyes bulged and darted around as he pressed his face between the iron rungs of the gate. Thick, foamy mucus dribbled from the sides of his mouth and a string of low, guttural sounds issued from deep within his throat. Fortwaith held something in his hands—a small, cloth-wrapped item, irregularly shaped and spattered with blood. He leaned forward through the bars and offered the parcel to the swab, his wild eyes becoming focused.

"I was wrong. Warn the others.

Lively approached cautiously, reaching out and taking the item from Fortwaith's outstretched hands. It was surprisingly heavy, made of either stone or metal, with pointy bits that required careful handling. He looked questioningly at Fortwaith and noticed that the man's face now bore a strange expression—a mixture of confusion and pain. Movement behind the captain caught Lively's eye, and he squinted into the darkness of the tunnel. Something glistened and moved back there. He leaned forward and peeked over Fortwaith's shoulder. From the center of the captain's back sprouted a thin, black tendril that swayed in and out of the shadows. It grew thicker down its length before disappearing into the darkness of the canal tunnel. Where the ropey tentacle made contact with Fortwaith, the man's shirt was soaked with blood—a crimson stain that was quickly spreading.

Stepping back fearfully, Lively looked again at Fortwaith's face. The man's confused expression had changed into one of dread. As Lively watched, Fortwaith's mouth opened and a rich, animal scream burst from his throat. It was the same sound that had echoed from deep within the city. Fortwaith grabbed the metal bars and shook them violently as his eyes and teeth receded backwards into his face. His features contorted into a pinched grimace before relaxing into an expressionless mask, his mouth and eye sockets now empty, black pits. Somehow the screams continued, accompanied now by a wet, sucking sound. Suddenly, from behind his own sloughed-off skin appeared Fortwaith's fleshy, howling face—lidless, lipless and apple-red. The black tentacle pulled taut, jerking his skinless body backwards and dragging him screaming into the darkness, a garish trail of blood smeared across the cobblestones in his wake. Like a discarded costume, the spongy, floppy mass of flesh and clothes that was his exterior collapsed between the bars in a wet tumble.

Lively opened his mouth and joined the captain's screams.

He back-peddled frantically from the horrific scene, his senses thrumming and his mind racing to make sense of what he saw. His screams became choked whimpers as he staggered drunkenly across the quay, pitching himself forward and into the rowboat with a reckless lunge. He landed hard, catching his wooden leg beneath the mast thwart and twisting as he fell. His face hit the wooden planks solidly. The small, cloth-wrapped object flew from his hands and across the boat, hitting the gunwale before landing on the bottom boards and rolling back towards him. As it rolled across the creaking planks the blood-spattered cloth unraveled behind it, revealing the object in full as it settled only inches from Lively's terrified face.

It was a pockmarked statuette cast in copper or possibly bronze, and covered in a mottled green patina. No larger than a clenched fist, it depicted an inhuman face with deep, cavernous eye sockets, black as tar, and dull, milk-white pearls glittering in the depths of each one. The thing's skin hung from its cheeks and jowls like old, soiled drapery and an inhumanly wide mouth split the sagging flesh there. The mouth gaped grotesquely, exposing random clusters of malformed teeth and a cavernous, fish-like gullet.

One last detail coaxed a soft, squeaky whimper from Lively. From within the creature's copper throat spilled dozens of strands of black seaweed. The putrescent tendrils poured from the thing's alien mouth in a waterfall of black, rotten strings. And at the end of each string dangled a small man, carved of bone and painted red.

At that moment something cold and wet brushed tentatively against Lively's back, and he closed his eyes

Tor stood upon the fo'c'sle of the anchored galley, rubbing his wrists and squinting across the river at the mouth of the canal. Still nothing.

An hour earlier, when the second set of screams had echoed from across the river, Branson decided to hell with orders and released Tor from the ship's hold. After unshackling the man and apologizing, he filled him in on what had transpired to the best of his knowledge. Tor nodded grimly. He too had heard the terrified shrieks from his cell, and could only surmise what dark fate befell Fortwaith and the others. The rest of the crew was wondering much the same, and were growing restless. To stay there much longer would surely mean a mutiny.

Branson stood on the deck nearby, eyeing Tor expectantly. "Sir?"

Tor waited another second or two, and then sighed heavily. "Weigh anchor."

Branson looked immensely relieved and quickly notified the rest of the crew, who set to quick work preparing the ship for departure. Soon enough the anchor was raised, and Yesterday glided slowly from the calm lagoon towards the river's channel, where the current would carry it south and back to familiar waters. Dozens of sailors hustled back and forth across the deck with newfound energy— tying off ropes, raising sails, and calling orders. Tor looked at the men, his men, and hoped he had made the right decision. He closed his eyes and whispered a silent prayer for the men they were leaving behind.

Just then a shrill cry echoed from the crow's nest.

"The dancers on the wall! They return!"

Tor opened his eyes and turned his gaze towards the city. Sure enough, there upon the wall were the crimson-clothed dancers, moving in convulsive rhythm and beckoning enigmatically. Tor found their movements to be hypnotic, but he shook his head clear and ordered his men to press on. As they put some distance between their ship and the city, it occurred to him that there were more dancers on the wall now than there were before. One dancer in particular caught his eye, the man's convulsive movements strangely peculiar and undeniably different than those of his kin. His dancing was erratic and he seemed to lurch and stagger while the others swayed gracefully. Tor walked along the rail, his eyes fixed on this strange dancer.

The galley had reached the channel by this point, and was moving along swiftly. Soon it would arrive at a great bend in the river that would take them out of sight of the city. Tor called to the lookout in the crow's nest, ordering him to come down. When he did, Tor ascended the mainmast himself. He climbed into the small bucket at the top. From his new vantage he could see more of the wall, and through a crumbled section much of the shadowy ruins beyond it. He focused his attention on that singular dancer. The boat reached the bend in the river, and as its course changed the moon slid behind the crimson dancers, outlining their silhouettes sharply in silvered light.

It was then that Tor understood why this one dancer moved so strangely. Below the dancer's left knee, where a leg should be, there was but a simple, wooden club.

Tor muttered an oath and fell back against the mainmast, gripping the iron rim of the crow's nest to steady himself. He tried to turn his head, but couldn't. As gruesome as the spectacle was, and as dark as the implications were, for some reason Tor could not pull his eyes away. He was mesmerized, and as he watched, the horrible truth of Rhomnus was revealed to him in full.

Tor saw that a black tendril emerged from the crippled dancer's back, from all of the dancers' backs, pulling and tugging at them like the strings of a puppeteer. The crimson forms danced in time with the tendrils' motions, their movements hauntingly synchronous with the undulating strands. Tor's fevered eyes followed the tendrils as they bloomed from the dancers' backs and rippled down the wall, growing thicker as they went. The tentacles, for that is what they now looked like, bulged and coiled like black intestines as they twisted through the ruined streets of Rhomnus. They grew in size and turgidity before finally sinking beneath the moonlit surface of a murky lake near the center of the city—a lake surrounded by a black, sandy beach and crumbling, marble temples. In the middle of the lake rose a massive, dome-shaped island—a pockmarked hill of greenish-grey that glistened wetly in the moonlight.

And as Tor watched from his swaying perch, the island shifted and opened its eyes.

TRACKS

LISA BUCKLEY

Her last sight was of hot blood melting into the cold snow next to her outstretched arm.

Gwen's waking world was of little better comfort. The choking panic, the sickening feeling of immobility—no, it was only her sleeping bag, and the unvoiced scream still stifling her breath. The fire in the soot-enameled wood stove had burnt low enough that moisture accumulated on the surface of her bag and had glazed the windows with frost. The watch on the sill glowed green—9pm. The sounds of the waking world slowly filtered into her consciousness: the snapping and popping of cold wood frames, the ragged sound of her breathing. The fear of the dream was still on her, and feeling of being hunted, chased, was hard to dispel. No matter. She was alone. Vigils are always solitary. Tracking nightmares was lonely work.

The sleeping bag no longer felt warm and comforting. She felt trapped, strangled. Gwen thrust it aside, and reached for her Miskatonic University sweatshirt. She sat up, leaning her arms on her knees, the heels of her hands in her eyes, her fingers clutching her head. She breathed slowly, tried to slow her heart rate. She needed tea, lots of tea, butwhat she really needed was for this nightmare to be over.

What most concerned Gwen was that her recent studies had put her on the radar of those people who needed no proof of the existence of cryptid beasts, or had their own fantastical interpretations. There was one local interest group called Weeden's Watchers with whom she had to eventually cut all contact. She had been put in touch with Weeden's Watchers by the librarian at MU. The Watchers were well-versed in both the history and the local legends of the settlement surrounding the University. Their collection of

1700s archives was far more extensive than those currently held at the university library, as many of the library's original archived correspondence were acquired by the Watchers after the recent downsizing. Subtle in their intensity, it soon became apparent that the Watchers' interests were not limited to their group's family connections with the events of the raid of April 12, 1771. No...no, it was too focused, and that focus was not only on validating the suspicions of Erza Weeden regarding the supposed necromantic activities of Joseph Curwen, and later with those of his doomed descendent. The Watchers eagerly sought the recovery of any artifact that would support that this necromancy was not only practiced, but was effective. They were convinced that these raised Dead stalked the woods to this day, and that the Dead—and they—had a mission to complete.

Gwen realized the sick obsession of the group only too late. She was invited on a nocturnal sojourn with the Watchers to the edges of the old potter's fields—the old outbuildings were now demolished, and the land sprouted a series of trappers' cabins in its place, and in one of these cabins she based her current work. She accompanied the group on their enthusiastic insistence that they needed her professional eye in identifying odd animal traces they had claimed to see in the woods surrounding the fields. These prints, described by the Watchers as large and predatory, piqued her interest: undocumented predatory creatures had plagued the bedevilled area since its settlement. However, the hunt for a flesh-and-blood track-maker soon degraded into a form of conjuring: invocations to "those whose rest was disturbed" and entreaties to the Disturbed to reveal the inner sanctum of their ancient tormentor. Disgusted and a concerned for her safety, Gwen melted into the woods under the cover of the dark, their frenzied chanting, and obsessive monitoring of infrared cameras. To this day Gwen did not know if they were aware of her departure that night: once again she changed her personal email and phone number and added yet another fanatical group to her black list.

The blighted roots of this perennial obsession crept deep in the soil of the community. The 1700s—specifically between 1690 to 1770—saw the beginnings of written reports of strange occurrences: missing trappers, brutalized livestock, daemonic eyes at windows, hunched shapes lurking in the shadows of outbuildings. The correspondence written by the townsfolk to their urban kin during the particularly harsh winters told of at least three gruesome murders during that period. The details did not reveal anything more than town gossip, as the first victims were foreigners and, therefore, already shunned by the superstitious and pious. However, the letters revealed that, after the brutal mauling of the hired hand of a respected farmer, a group of men undertook a "Hunt for a Most Ravenous Wilde Beast of the Woods" in the spirit of protecting "all Good and Decent Citizens of The Towne." When the men of the hunt returned from their three day journey with the bodies of several coyotes and one mountain lion, the official word was that this Beast was dealt with: mountain lions are known to both skin and eviscerate their kills.

The official decree did nothing to stop the festering terror and paranoia of the townspeople, which always peaked around the times of the old festivals of Walpurgis and All Hallow's Eve. Reports subsided after the razing of the suspected necromancer Curwen's property in 1771, but the repressed collective memory of the Beast slowly bubbled to the surface of the regional consciousness like an oily film in the early 1900s, when the noisome bubbles burst again. Time had lore-transformed the Beast into a familiar of the Black Man, harvesting victims whose blood was used in unspeakable rites within the white ring of stones, served in a leaden bowl to the chaotic piping of shrill flutes. The link between the Beast and the Black Man was alluded to in A History of Mathematical Sorcery in the Miskatonic River Valley, written by Frank Elwood during his leave of absence from the University in 1928 after the death of his roommate, Gilman, by inexplicable circumstances in a boarding house with ties to the witch trials. The boarding house was once the ghastly abode—and the site of countless murders of children sacrificed to the Black Man—for the witch Keziah Mason and her abhorrent primate familiar. Elwood published his roommate's findings against the recommendations of his psychiatrists and to the detriment of his academic career.

Elwood's fantastical conjectures of numberless bestial entities living in catacombs beneath all places of habitation and burial revealed his own macabre obsession. The youth had been enamoured with the contemporary works of Pickman before the artist's sudden and mysterious disappearance in 1926. One cannot look upon Pickman's nightmarish creations without permanently scarring one's mind, and Gwen was no exception. While investigating the possible source lore of the Beast, Gwen had come across a photocopy of a snapshot taken of Pickman's "Ghoul Feeding." The precision of the anatomical detail of the hellish carnivore was so life-like, so alive, that the subject crawled from the imperfect copy she held and burrowed deep into her subconscious. That night, and any night thereafter during times of stress, she dreamt of awakening in her apartment, awakening only to be immobilized with fear, awakening to see the fiend hunched at the foot of her bed, fixing her with its charnel red gaze, the moonlight silvering its bared, grinning teeth.

In the three centuries of sightings, speculation as to the Beast's identity had vacillated between the physical and the metaphysical. The manner in which the livestock and human corpses were found—skinned, flesh torn and removed—caused scholars to attribute the accounts to mass-hysteria associated with a much earlier mythology: local Native American groups claimed the Beast was the cult-perverted version of their legend of the Wendigo, the physical embodiment and cautionary tale of madness and cannibalism brought about by the harsh winter climes. The similarities between oral histories of the Wendigo and those of the Beast were uncanny: humanoid yet bestial, existing on the edges of humanity, the flayed remains of its victims the only trace. Wendigo lore no doubt fanned the flames of the hearth-side fears of the European Christian community, while the activities of black souls in Arkham and Salem only confirmed their suspicions of the arcane horrors that existed on the dark fringes of their world. These urban legends were preserved by the codgers and dowagers of the town, flatly dismissed by the University, and rabidly believed by the paranormal groups. Not all that died, the old timers said, remained at rest, and secrets that were better left as dust were rebuilt. Of course, when pressed for details, the old-timers blathered frustratingly incoherent tales that blended the reality of the forest with tales of lichcraft.

The myth of the Beast followed the familiar pattern of any report of a cryptid animal: a legend of ancient origin, pre-dating or coinciding with the arrival of Europeans. Continuously sighted by those locals and tourists but never documented; briefly seen and quickly exaggerated. Some say it was raised by the Watchers—now rumored to possess several ancient tomes of spellcraft that once belonged to the University—to hunt the descendants of its tormentors. Some say it seeks the graves that were fresh and plentiful over a century ago, and that Pickman was nothing more than a wildlife artist of the grave. Some say it was defending its ancestral territory—yet talk is not proof. How can something be so regularly seen and leave no trace? It cannot, if it exists outside of the realm of hysteria and madness.

Not once had a search for the Beast been conducted using the scientific method, and the study of this legend was similar enough to her previous work in dispelling wildlife legends that the proposal to her graduate committee seemed logical. The Beast was said to roam more widely during the winter months to sate its abominable appetites. Winter meant snow. Snow meant footprints. Footprints, both fossil and modern, had been the focus of her career these ten years past. After the debacle with the Watchers, Gwen vowed to focus the lens of science on this case and forever exorcise the fiend that leered in her dreams. Given the lengths to which the PR departments at Miskatonic University went to distance the school from its more eccentric alumni and to downplay its ancient cabalistic archives, Gwen assumed that her committee would be pleased. They were not pleased. Both committee and department considered her proposal to track the Beast an extra-curricular activity at best, career suicide at worst. No matter: Gwen was determined to either find this Beast, or banish it forever from the realm of her nightmares.

Gwen stoked the last embers in the woodstove. Light from the near-full moon slanted coyly through the frosted glass of the small trapper's cabin. A late-evening breakfast by the dying embers while she reviewed her notes of the previous days. Several cups of black tea washed the uneasy shrouds of the dream from her mind. The brutal cold had kept local folk close by their fires and away from Potter's field for the last two weeks, so the only human tracks within 20 km of her cabin had been those of her own snowshoes. The tenants of the potter's field received no visitors: sometimes what is gone is truly forgotten.

Gwen knew these woods and their local fauna intimately. Her notes detailed the constant presence of rabbits, squirrels, weasels, deer, elk, fox, coyote, wolf, mountain lion, raven, owl: all these traces were documented, and their patterns of form and behaviour were comfortably predictable. If nothing else, her findings would make for an interesting report on the activities of the winter inhabitants of the river valley. What she was searching for on her transects through the snow-muted woods was the unpredictable: a trackway of a known animal so distorted by movement, time, or deformity as to be mistaken by the lore-converted as the otherworldly Beast: a local with a penchant for frightening his neighbours (or increasing the paranormal tourist trade), a sick bear, awake when all bears should be hibernating, a mange-rattled dog or coyote. Or merely nothing, nothing at all: figments and phantoms of a region suckled for centuries on terror and darkness.

Fog clung to the trunks of the porcelain trees when Gwen started her evening transect. The meat left at the bait posts was removed under the cover of dark, although the few motion cameras she could afford either caught fog or were found inactive the following mornings. No clear tracks or traces surrounded the bait posts, only drag marks and scuffled snow. Foxes, coyotes, and the occasional wolf came to investigate the remnants of frozen blood, but the cameras that still functioned captured their arrival without fault. Whoever was tampering with her cameras and her bait was going to great lengths to remain unseen. Her own transect paths were so hard-packed that it was impossible to tell if she was being followed. So she waited for the next hint of snow, baited her stations afresh, and waited for the snow to subside. Tonight was a clean slate. Gwen donned her down parka, laced up her snowshoes, and loaded her camera and documenting gear into her pack.

Gwen set out around midnight. She was tired. This chase was taking its toll on her psyche, and the thought of someone tampering with her work gnawed at her nerves. Every night since her arrival at the cabin she awoke in a cold sweat, haunted by graphic images of blood and fear, fresh hot blood melting into the snow next to her arm. The images slid beneath the surface of her consciousness, and rippled her thoughts just enough to remind her of their presence. Gwen was embarrassed at her unease. This self-imposed sabbatical was supposed to be relaxing. She'd never been nervous in the field before, but the solitude coupled with the local legends were enough to tax any mind.

The contours of the freshly white-scaped land were thrown into sharp contrast in the moonlight. The snow twinkled and squeaked underfoot. The stars glowed cold and distant. It would be a good night, Gwen thought. She set off along her predetermined bearing, across the corner of the burial grounds and into the far woods. Her total trip would be 10km there and back, with most of her return trip completed after sunrise. She would reach her bait station right after it was picked clean, or (with luck) she would catch the thief in action.

Gwen was both annoyed and elated to see the fresh set of snowshoe tracks heading in the direction of the bait station. I have you now, bastard, she thought. I will see you. Your ass is mine. Confrontation didn't worry her. Based on the size of the snowshoe imprints she knew she was dealing with someone roughly her size, and she would be a formidable match for them, man or woman.

She followed the tracks for another kilometer, and saw that a second set of tracks were following the first. A footprint type she had never before encountered was imprinted clearly next to one of the perpetrator's prints. Looking east she saw that the newcomer had entered the woods back in the direction of the cemetery. On encountering the perpetrator's tracks, the newcomer had stooped—maybe to catch a scent. A forelimb and hind limb print were clear. New newcomer must have suffered from a horrible illness or deformity that affected the limbs—as large as that of an adult male human, yet the fingers and toes were elongate and sharply pointed, terminating in uneven claws. They reminded her of bear tracks, sometimes so human as to be misidentified, yet too mis-proportioned, too long of limb and foot to be those of a healthy bear. The track-maker then rose and followed the snowshoe tracks. Gwen knew she should stop and document the traces, but she also knew that she joined a chase in progress. There was no time, not if she wanted to see the animal responsible for the tracks.

Its gait was inconsistent, now running on two limbs, now trotting on four. It stopped occasionally, crouching next to the snowshoe prints as if to examine them. It crouched like a man, but no man could lay claim to such limbs, and no rubber forgery could reproduce such detail. Then it rose and resumed its chase. It moved quickly. And it was not alone.

At the four kilometer mark two more bestial trails joined the first. Gwen became nervous and edgy. While she had fantasized about assailing the person once overtaking him, it seemed he may now be in real danger. He must have also sensed his danger: the pace of the snowshoes quickened. She picked up her pace to match that of the hunted.

The dull silence and the rapid crunch-squeak of snow were shattered by a howl, not that of a dog or a wolf, but a baying, screaming cry. Her Companion, as she now thought of him, had stopped here as well. Had he also heard that cry, a sound that knotted insides and chilled skin once warm with exertion? The cry came from everywhere: behind, beside, ahead. Ahead. Fighting every instinct that screamed turn and run, just run, it was ahead she must go if there was any chance of helping the person. Her Companion had also started to run, but it would do no good, not with snowshoes, not with the three now surging ahead without pause, without any break in stride. Gwen pushed herself forward.

There. Behind her. Yes, she was sure this time. That was no trick of the woods. There was something following her now. The cold air carried sound so crisply it could be 100m or 1000m away. Feet in the snow. Fast feet. Running. Close. Running. Run. Run dammit...

Running forward. No thoughts of rescue now. She surges ahead, rasping in cold air, growling out the lungs' exhaust...the growling is behind her now.

She no longer looks down to follow the Companion. She aims for the clearing before her station. There are tools there...something lay there...

Her Companion didn't make it. At the base of the bait tree is a body, once in parka and hood, now bare to the elements. It is the epicenter of a halo of pink-dyed snow, tainted purple with the moon. Blood and tissue are trampled into the packed ring. They had torn into him with relish. The denuded blue-grey bones of the ribcage swirl in sick contrast with the parka-clad limbs. The body is still steaming. Stumbling forward, she looks. The face, who was he...who...

The face, streaked with blood, no, the face, her face, her blood, her face, attached to the flayed gutted steaming torso, intact, so still, still her face, no no, the gagging scream rose but would not come, but they are coming now, she turns to see, gagging and choking, her quarry, the three carnivorous fiends, human yet not, faces twisted with the charnel veil of the pit, jaws, eyes that stared at her every night, that see death beyond death, eyes once fixed and staring like her eyes, her eyes, staring into her own eyes, her own death stare...

Her last sight was of hot blood melting into the cold snow next to her outstretched arm.

CHEAP VODKA SAVES THE WORLD

S.M. OKEYB

Not for the first time, Danny was glad he had done acid in college. Thanks to that pharmaceutical experimentation, his mind had some practice accepting things that simply ought not to be. Consequently he had not just pissed himself and gibbered when things that could not reasonably exist began crawling out of that pit in the center of the chamber. Certainly all the other rules and assumptions on which Danny had based his life had for the past few years proved increasingly false and ineffectual, so it was only logical that hideous beasts crawling from industrial chasms would not conform to the laws of Darwinian adaptation. And what evolutionary advantage could a bipedal creature possibly gain by having human heads where its hands ought to be? Consider how useful his own hands now proved, for example—one to hold the knife, and one to stanch the bleeding.

The other bums (yes, the other bums, for he must count himself among them, master's degree or not) had warned him not to sleep there, but Danny had walked away smiling. He knew the island had once been a Civil War prison and that thousands had died there. This accounted for the old timers' skittishness more than anything, he had figured, for the chronically homeless were often superstitious. Possibly the old hydro-plant was plagued by supernatural terror, but far more likely the old drunks who had vanished simply fell in the river after one drink too many, an easy feat given the lay of the place and the gaps in the floor.

Now Danny was glad for their warning, because it meant possibly he had not gone entirely insane himself. It reassured him to know that when a garden gnome had crawled out of that hole with a straight razor, it did NOT prove the total mental breakdown he'd feared since hitting the streets. Something was in there with him.

Getting to the inner chamber meant crawling through a porthole roughly two feet wide, set chest high in a concrete wall—in itself a formidable task for your typical vagrant. Once inside, there was a queen-sized slab of stone beneath this porthole to sleep upon, the rest of the room being filled with water that flowed into the massive hole at the chamber's center, and presumably drained to the river below. Danny could not confirm this without getting his shoes wet, something no homeless person wanted to do. He saw, though, that the hole was ringed with steel and rusted bolts.

No one was likely to climb down the concrete walls to bother him, but he had strung some scavenged wire across the porthole, wrapping it from bolt to bolt like a child forming a star. Anyone breaking through that was bound to make noise, and his six-inch survival knife would be more than enough for any hands or heads poked through, if it came to that. Most likely a good rap with the fist or a stray bit of concrete or rebar would do.

Still chuckling at the fear in the veteran vagrants' faces, Danny had lain across his unrolled sleeping bag, backpack and a folded towel for a pillow, the sheathed knife beneath them. Fall's first frosts had killed the mosquitoes, but tonight was warm and ought to have been as good as any to be without a roof. With the streetlights on not too far away, he could see quite well, and he felt certain the place was secure. Yet he felt jittery, like a man who's just been told he's swallowed poison, then slapped on the back and assured it was only a joke. Phantom pains and cramps slid through his body as he lay down to sleep. Dark, savage thoughts seemed to flit through his mind like wolves through a forest.

Assuring himself that the old timers had gotten to him, Danny stretched his limbs deliberately, lay back once again, and summoned a vision of his favorite barista at the coffee shop where he bummed change out front on the lunch hour.

His conscious mind was just drifting away from the prolonged, delectable seduction he envisioned when he suddenly somehow had her in the woods, pulling off her pants to find the lass unkempt beneath them, peeking closer and finding not hairs, but tiny red worms writhing free from her pores like meat from a grinder.

He woke up gagging, nearly tipping into the water as he shot upright. Gasping, he took a moment to assure himself he was awake, and was reaching for the vodka in his pack when a specter of his youth appeared. As a teen, Danny had heard of people playing pranks by stealing a garden gnome before a road trip, then returning the gnome with pictures of it in famous places, posed before various landmarks. But by the look of it, if this gnome had ever been kidnapped, it was returned to its grateful owners with a packet of photos showing it gang-raped by mandrills, or tortured with power tools, and had promptly stabbed the family to death with kitchen knives and knitting needles.

It wore the typical pointy red hat and thick white beard, having no practical need for the straight razor it slowly unfolded. Looking exactly like one from a row out front of the hardware store except, of course, for being apparently alive and giddily homicidal, it goggled and drooled at him, wading steadily through water up to its thighs. High school karate lessons still serving him well, Danny waited as it approached the stone on which he stood, then kicked the terrible thing squarely in the gut. Tramping around for a year with a full pack had muscled his legs up nicely, and he heard the gratifying metallic clang above the rushing water as it flew back into the pit, banging against the further side and into the deepening darkness. It did not return.

Danny found himself smiling. He'd long grown tired of the whole goddamned world, but here was something interesting, something real. Fantastic as it may be, it seemed far more real than the world of cotton-clad consumers just a quarter-mile away. Of course, nothing strictly impossible had occurred, but he felt certain that it would. A bad dream was just a bad dream, after all, and it was conceivably possible that a very little man with a passion for finely-edged implements had happened to dwell in a pit within an overgrown hydroelectric station. Highly unlikely, of course, and what next crawled forth convinced him that something wholly inhuman was happening.

Gnomes had been a part of his childhood. For a while in primary school, he'd been obsessed with them, had been teased about them at school, and he felt certain that the murderous irony of this youthfully-adored icon was meant to terrify him. Whatever force he faced was inside his mind, grubbing through his memories for weakness. Certainly the giant roach suggested this.

For that was what came next, crawling forelegs and feelers first out of the water, five feet long and dripping wet and glistening in the distant light. It was not simply an up-scaled *Periplaneta americana*—its mandibles were more fearsome than Danny remembered, and it was able to rear back like a mantis, hissing and gnashing its jaws, wide enough to put his fist into. Danny smirked.

In sixth grade he had had a terrible phobia of bugs, owing to a particular film he should not have been allowed to watch. But this, too, was a relic of the past. In his time as a tramp he had awoken many times with bugs upon him, brushing them off like autumn leaves. Now this ridiculous oversize arthropod, hissing and flailing its chitinous limbs at him, did not frighten or repulse him, but filled his mind with happy thoughts of how, precisely, he might destroy it.

Hoisting his pack like a shield before him, left arm slung through the straps, gripping the furthest one tightly, Danny stepped down into the water and splashed toward the scuttling thing, bending his knees as he shoved the pack at its face, letting its mandibles dig into his dirty clothes and second-hand books. With its jaws sunk fast, Danny pushed up from the ground with all his might, strong legs serving him again, hoisting the beast upright, baring the yellow, segmented belly to his stabbing, slashing steel.

It was over far too quickly—less than a minute, he reckoned, and the freakish thing fell still. Danny found some consolation in crushing its head against the wall with his boot—the only way, apparently, to open its jaws and free his pack. Some of his clothes were shredded, and he wouldn't be finishing Grapes of Wrath or the New Testament anytime soon, but his camp stove and fuel were intact, two portable miracles for a bum with winter on the way. Hell, he'd only taken that Bible for kindling anyhow. The shelter passed them out the way he wished they passed out sandwiches.

It had been ages since he'd used his body in self-defense, and some deep instinct awoke with a savage glee. Part of his mind begged him to unwrap the wire and get out of there, part of his mind warned that any attempt to crawl out of that tiny portal would leave him vulnerable to attack, and part of his mind urged him to stay right there and kick every bit of ass that he possibly could.

He imagined himself saving humanity from some fledgling supernatural force, or the vanguard of some alien invasion, not from love of his fellow man, but merely because the poor damn beast had made itself a target for the rage inside him—rage at his own species, who seemed content to let him starve and die when a dollar would work miracles, who laid him off after decades of work so some overpaid suit could still get his bonus when profits flagged. His fingers flexed around the knife. He felt fear, it was true, but his rage destroyed it. Hell, he considered killing himself everyday.

Two down now, and he was still untouched. Danny shook his head and smiled. It would shit-sure have to do better than a goddamned garden gnome and a giant cockroach. Maybe next will be a femme fatale or two, he mused—perhaps some bikini models with vampire toes and *vagina dentata*. If the thing kept to its telepathic tricks, it would have to be a good-looking female, for once he hit puberty few things had so terrified Danny as a beautiful woman.

Opening his pack, he pulled the fuel canister out, wrapped his towel around it and pushed it to the bottom of the pack, surprising himself with some provisions for the future—for even a bum who saves the world would still get cold in the winter. Pulling the Zippo from his shirt pocket, he flicked on the flame and took a look around—not, it must be admitted, into the pit, though his shoes and pants were soaked by now, but around the shallow water in the chamber. Finding a few lengths of rebar and some good-sized chunks of concrete, he lay these down on the stone where he had tried to sleep.

More preparations had crossed his mind, but just then the first fist of the head-handed monster appeared—splashing onto the rim of the pit like an idiot peeking over a fence, moving up on an impossibly long neck soon becoming a forearm, the rest of the beast rising slowly into view, seeming distinctly (and disconcertingly) to have been pushed upward.

It was hideous to see, certainly. Danny wondered again if his opponent's goal was, in fact, to scare him off so it might be about its business. It was a human form, with hairy chest and arms, and an absurd penis dangling at its crotch, but lacking a head in the proper place and, instead, with forearms thick as necks, had a full-sized head where each hand ought to be. Its two idiot faces eyed Danny like dim, cruel children cornering a cat. He wondered if it meant to chew him to death.

He heaved a rock left-handed, the knife in his right, and the damned thing moved fast, jerking the right face away, but taking a hit to the chest. Lunging after the stone, Danny hoped to sink the knife in its heart as it reeled, but its left arm swung up and sank teeth into his lower ribs, the force of the blow knocking his blade so it bounced off the sternum, leaving a long gash behind it. The beast drew back, and Danny felt a chunk of his flesh go with it, saw the left face slaver it down through bare, ragged teeth. A cold wave of fear rippled through him, then passed and dispersed.

Shoving his pack to his left, he raised his knife on his right, blocking one face, slashing the other, opening a wound across the eyes, slashing blindly to the left now, catching that one above the ear, slashing again to the right, opening that one's cheek, back and forth, slashing right and left and blocking with the pack it was chewing to pieces. Finally, the left-face, half-blinded by blood, flaps of flesh hanging loosely in all directions, clamped onto his forearm with a terrible strength. Fist Face (as even now his mind had named it) heaved him back against the wall, red furrows rising on his arm as he slumped below the porthole.

Stunned by the impact, Danny dropped the pack beside him, heard the clash of his knife on the stone, heard Fist Face stalking toward him. The sounds entered his mind as through butter—thickly and slowly. Groping through blurred vision and blackened vision, he got both hands on the longest length of rebar just in time to strike a wide, swinging blow at the creature's right head, just a hair above the brow.

Never was the crack of a grand slam bat half so glorious. Though the brains did not erupt, the skull split with a thick, pulpy sound and that half of the beast went still as if paralyzed by a stroke, knee dropping limply to the ground. Danny watched Fist Face struggle to stay upright, grinned at its lurching helplessness and useless right side. He took his time lining up the next shot, and was pleased by the yellowish bits that spurted through the fissure he made across the intact cranium.

Bleeding above a bested opponent, Danny bellowed as the rebar clattered on the stone beneath him, "That all you got? Can't do better than a giant bug and a man with faces for fists?" With new found pride in his species, he yelled as loudly as he could, hoping also to reach the human ears on the distant shore, "You're gonna have to do better than that to take on the human race! We ain't all fat slobs and crazy old drunks. Hell, there's plenty of people out there a whole lot tougher than ME!

"C'mon, ya bastard send me something good, somethin' with fangs and teeth like a proper nightmare. Hell, face me yourself, ya damned freak! Or maybe ya can't. Maybe you're some wee little thing I could kill with my piss..."

Hearing no noises, Danny sank tiredly and sat, digging clothes from his pack. It reeked of naphtha—Fist Face must have broken his fuel cylinder through the towel. His 100 proof vodka, in its glorious plastic, was wholly unbroken, and Danny helped himself to some internal and external infusions. Then he heard the sounds.

Between squelching and scraping, between crashing and cracking, the sounds rumbled up from the pit like harbingers of hell. Danny stuffed the bottle back in his pack, not thinking to cap it, his mouth agape with wonder. The ground shook as he stumbled to his feet, holding his knife in one hand, pressing an ancient t-shirt to his chest wound with the other.

He was not disappointed. A huge, horrible form loomed up from the abyss, not so much rising as assembling itself bit by bit. Giant legs sunk deep in the pit, it was manlike but for its huge, four-horned head and bestial face, made all the more ghastly by its vestigial humanity, with arms as big as tree trunks, legs like Doric columns. It leered down upon him, baring fangs like a masochist's knives. Something like a smile split its face like a splatter of blood.

"Now THAT," thought Danny with some satisfaction as it swooped down upon him, "is a fucking MONSTER!"

His smile remained even as talons long and thick as railroad spikes drove into his stomach. His eyes and brain processed the motion only as a faint, lingering trail in the aftermath. In the impact one limp hand fell upon and clutched at his tattered pack and contents. Danny felt a splash on his face as the uncapped vodka sloshed about inside it, dribbling down the side as the fiend hoisted him upward, its grisly maw expanding to accommodate him. Inside shone row upon row of small, rending teeth. Nearly amused by the pain filtering through the shock of impalement, Danny thought to himself, Cheap vodka saves the world!

And he shoved the pack straight in its mouth. The rasping, ravenous teeth snapped it up eagerly, but not eagerly enough to stop him tossing his lit Zippo in after it. That pack was sodden with 100 proof booze and naphtha, with nothing inside but paper and cotton, and it went down flaming to the belly of the beast.

Inside the pit where he had fallen and floated, Danny lived just long enough see tongues of light and smoke spilling from cracks across the creature's surface, like a knight aflame inside his armor.

Two months later, when another traveling vagabond arrived and wondered why the other homeless folks shunned such a cozy hideaway, he too scoffed at the horror stories. Settling in with a bottle and a battered guitar, he sang sad songs till midnight, loving the chamber's acoustics.

In the morning, he emerged refreshed, having forgotten the old timers' warnings, and set about getting to Memphis.

THE DRINKER OF SOULS

SEAN P. ROBSON

When I first met Gaston he was slumped against his coach, surrounded by the bodies of the bandits who ambushed him, his left hand pressed tight against his abdomen to keep his entrails from falling out, and coughing up frothy pink blood. Given the severity of his wounds, I expected him to die in the night, not live on to become one of my closest friends.

The Ardennes is no place to travel lightly, especially not in these times. It is said that the Enlightenment will free the world from the shackles of superstition, but the brightest flames cast the darkest shadows, and evil still lurks in the deep and quiet places of the Earth. So I was wary when the sounds of battle—the ring of gunshots, the screams of anger and of pain, and the clash of steel on steel—drew me to the clearing in the gloom of the late afternoon's dying light. A more prudent man would have hurried on his way, happy to steer clear of bloody conflict, but I have never counted prudence among my virtues, though curiosity is chief among my vices.

Hidden in shadow at the edge of the clearing, I saw the fallen tree that blocked the road, the black coach with its whinnying, frightened horses, and its driver slumped dead on the seat, feathered with crossbow bolts. I saw the bandits who rushed forth to claim their prize, and the snarling, cursing, raging man who contested their claim. The man's clothes were of the finest cut, and the quality of his sword was obvious even at a distance. A brace of pistols lay discarded at his feet near the bodies of the first two bandits to charge in. He fought like a cornered wolf, parrying each thrust of the three remaining attackers and lashing out viciously whenever they came too near. The fletching of a crossbow bolt protruded from between his ribs on his left side, and he was breathing with obvious difficulty. The dogs would soon have him and both he and they knew it. Yet he did not ask for quarter, and I doubt he would have accepted had it been offered. Instead, he defied his attackers and prepared to sell his life as dearly as possible.

I left the cover of shadow and walked quickly and quietly across the clearing, unnoticed by the combatants until I slid the point of my poignard into the right kidney of one of the bandits, and then pulled it out and stepped aside as he fell, bleeding out like a stuck pig.

The momentary distraction of my intervention gave the lone defender the opening he needed. He thrust his sword quick as a striking snake, past the bandit's guard and into his chest. Unfortunately the man's blade stuck and he was unable to withdraw it before the last remaining bandit slashed him across the belly. The man staggered backward and grasped the side of the coach, leaning heavily on it to stay on his feet.

The bandit turned to face me—too late—I was already inside the reach of his sword, and I drove my poignard under his chin, through his soft palate and into his brain.

"Well fought, monsieur," I said, turning to the mortally wounded man, whose ragged breath fogged in the chill autumn air. He coughed and spit up blood, then slid slowly to the ground, holding his stomach. I knelt beside him and pressed my wine skin to his lips. "My name is Falcone," I said.

"Gaston, Comte de Reims," he said, drinking deeply, which set off another fit of laboured coughing.

"You have great courage," I said. "But I am afraid your wounds are mortal. There is nothing I can do to help you, except... ease your passing?" I gestured with my bloody knife.

Gaston looked at me and smiled weakly. "Not just yet, I think," he said. "If I am to die let it be in my own home, not on some nameless forest road surrounded by the bodies of swine." He gestured to the dead bandits. "My estate is not far. If you would consent to take me there, I would be even more deeply in your debt than I already am. Can you drive the team?" I admitted that I could and consented to grant the dying man his wish, though I doubted he would live long enough to make it home. After clearing away the dead-fall I helped Gaston into the coach and made him as comfortable as was possible, and following his directions, I set the coach on its way to Reims.

Despite Gaston's assurance that his home was not far, nightfall found us still in the wilds. I resisted the impulse for haste, and slowed the horses to a walk rather than risking an upset in the dark. The coach's lantern cast a wan light on the road ahead that merely enhanced the claustrophobic clutch of the night-dark woods, which seemed to unnaturally amplify the clip-clop of the horse's hooves and Gaston's wheezing gasps. I uttered a brief prayer to Hecate, mistress of the crossroads, and pressed on through the nocturnal gloom.

It was well past midnight when we finally arrived at Gaston's estate, and, though the hour was late and I was a stranger, the drowsy gate keeper admitted us at once when I told him of the Comte's plight. He roused the household, and servants quickly whisked their master, who continued to defy death as stubbornly as he had his attackers, to his rooms where they cared for him behind closed doors, while I gratefully retired to a guest room.

The next morning I was summoned to Gaston's side, and I was amazed by the improvement in his condition; his colour had returned and he was breathing without difficulty. It hardly seemed possible that this was the same man who had clung to a gossamer-thin strand of life only hours earlier.

Gaston took my hand in his. "Falcone, you risked your own life for that of stranger and if not for your timely succor I would now be naught but a feast for crows. You must surely be the heaven-sent agent of my deliverance."

"Hardly that," I said. "My arrival in your moment of need was merely a fortunate coincidence. The true miracle is that you survived wounds that should surely have killed you."

"Perhaps, but the miracle, if you wish to call it that, was not of my making," Gaston said. I glanced about the room and saw a bowl of unguent next to a mortar-and-pestle and jars of sulphur, mercury, and salt sitting on a nearby table. Next to them sat a leather-bound book entitled *Archidoxa*. "Ah, Paracelsus," I said.

Gaston raised an eyebrow in surprise. "You are an alchemist, Falcone?"

"I've dabbled in the art," I said. "Among other things."

"But this is wonderful!" Gaston exclaimed. "You must stay here as my guest and keep me company while I convalesce; we can discuss natural philosophy, and you will enjoy my library, I am sure."

"I have no business more pressing," I said. "I would be delighted to accept your hospitality."

And so I became a permanent fixture in the Comte's estate. I entertained Gaston with tales of my travels from one end of the Empire to the other, sitting first by his bedside, then later when he was well enough, in his library. He did not exaggerate the scope of his book collection, which by itself spoke to his vast wealth, for it contained copies of nearly every important contemporary work of natural and occult philosophy as well as many rare and ancient ones. We ensconced ourselves each day in his library reading, drinking, and talking until the candles were melted stubs and the glimmer of dawn cracked the veil of night. We studied the magical formulae dictated by Trithemius and Albertus Magnus, debated the hermetic principles of

Paracelsus, and of course the occult philosophy of Agrippa; and week by week, month by month, as autumn passed to winter and then turned its eyes to spring, our friendship grew. Gaston recognized in me a kindred spirit whose thirst for knowledge and power rivalled his own. In his workshop we brewed the *aqua vitae* of Abulcasis, tried our hands at minor incantations, and held discourse with spirits who answered the call of sorcery.

Late one night in April as the hours of darkness retreated before the coming of Walpurgisnacht, and Gaston and I were deep in our cups and thick in conspiracy, he showed me a book that I had not previously seen in his collection, ancient and mouldering with crumbling vellum pages scribed in rust-brown ink. Upon the badly worn cover the title, *Nox Veneficus*, was barely visible. I handled the fragile tome with the greatest care as I slowly perused the pages written in cramped Latin. The book described various *magna incantata*, along with the names and rites by which the major entities of the Dark Beyond might be summoned. Possession of this book alone was heresy and carried a sentence of death, and I realized the great trust I had earned for Gaston to show it to me.

"This one looks interesting," I said, indicating a spell to summon a creature called The Drinker of Souls. "Shall we try it?"

I looked up at Gaston and was surprised to see him pale and trembling, staring fixated at the page. "No, Falcone," he whispered. "Not for all the money in the world. Not again.

"Again?"

"How ironic that you should suggest the only spell in this book that I have tried, and I wish with all my soul that I had not."

I refilled Gaston's snifter from the decanter of cognac on the table. "You must tell me about it," I said, pulling my chair close to his by the fireplace. The light from the fire cast dancing shadows across his face, masking his expression as he sipped from his glass.

"Years ago, while attending university in Burgundy, I happened to attend Agrippa's lectures, and it was there that I first met my friends Phillipe, Manfred, Bernardo, and Michel, who were, like me, burdened with equal measures of wealth and boredom. The ideas that Agrippa proposed were outrageous, so of course they peaked our interest. We five formed a cabal born of ennui and convened nightly to study occult principles and get drunk. Several of the works we read mentioned a profane book of forbidden knowledge, *Nox Veneficus*, and we became obsessed with obtaining it. We haunted the libraries of the major universities of France and the Empire searching for the book's whereabouts, and eventually we traced it to a private library in Constantinople.

"And so we traveled there, all five of us, confident that we could entice the owner, a scholar named Aydin Sadik, to sell it. Although he received us graciously enough, he adamantly refused to part with the book despite the considerable sums we offered. Sadik refused to even let us read its pages, insisting that its contents were too dangerous to be shared. This inflamed our desire for the book all the more, and I am ashamed to confess that we resorted to murder and theft when negotiation failed. While Phillipe and I tried to reason with the man, Bernardo, always impatient, approached Sadik from behind and brought a heavy bronze bust of Constantine down upon his head. We never meant to kill him, but there he lay at our feet, skull crushed and eyes bulging, casting defiance in the teeth of our intent.

"At that moment, though, our only care was for the book; for the knowledge and power that was ours for the taking. We quickly returned to our rented rooms, where, drunk on victory and too much arak, we performed the very ritual you suggested. We summoned the Drinker of Souls. What hubris to think that such callow novices as ourselves could bind and control such a creature! We had no offering to appease it, so instead it took Bernardo, who had led the ritual. It drank him dry and then, with no wards to constrain it, it fled into the night, set loose upon the world by our reckless ignorance. The remaining four of us returned home and attempted to put the past behind us, hoping that we had seen the last of the demon. But the thing was not done with us; it had taken human form and needed to feed upon the souls of those who summoned it to prolong its own earthly existence. The years passed and, one by one, my friends were taken until finally, ten years ago Michel, the last of us left besides me, was found in his study, vacant-eyed and drooling—a mindless husk. And so the book, which had been in his possession, passed to me."

"Ten years," I said. "How have you managed to elude the demon for so long?"

Gaston smiled. "By placing my soul out of reach. It is safeguarded and he shall never have it."

"Surely, Gaston, you haven't turned to religion in your desperation? The Christians promise salvation, but you know as well as I that it is an empty promise."

Gaston snorted in contempt. "Hardly," he said. "Falcone, I have something to show you." He pulled himself out of his chair, unsteady from too much drink. In front of a large bookcase beneath a bust of Pallas was a thick Persian rug, which Gaston pulled aside. Beneath it was a trap door in the floor that was so cleverly made that it was difficult to see even when uncovered. Taking an oil lamp from a side table, Gaston lifted the trap door and descended into the hidden chamber, beckoning me to follow. He led me down the stone steps into a small chamber excavated from the manor's foundation.

"An old cellar, dug generations ago, meant to hide the family treasures should the estate ever fall to raiders," he said. "But I've found a better use for it." The cramped cellar looked like a necromancer's workshop from Bosch's darkest imaginings: a stained altar stood before a pentagram etched into the floor. Human skulls served as candelabras, and a shelf held several other books as dark and profane as *Nox Veneficus*, itself. Gaston pulled out a loose stone on the wall and from its cavity he withdrew a silver filigreed flask etched with arcane runes.

"When I said my soul was protected," he said, "I meant something more certain than the vague assurances of the Pope. When I transferred my soul into this phylactery, I not only thwarted the demon that hunts me, but also the ravages of time, itself. I have achieved what only a handful of sorcerers ever have—immortality. And should my body ever be destroyed it would be no difficult matter to claim a new one."

I suddenly wondered if Gaston might have had an ulterior motive for wanting me to take him home when he was critically injured. Perhaps Gaston read something in my glance, because he quickly put the flask back in its hiding place and replaced the rock that concealed it.

"Of course it may just be baseless superstition," he said with a laugh that sounded forced. He placed his hand on my back and urged me back upstairs to the library, whence we said our good nights and retired to our bed chambers.

Things were different between Gaston and me after that night, and our friendship began to deteriorate. Our conversation, once animated and lively, was now punctuated with many awkward silences and I often caught Gaston casting sullen glances at me. We bickered and sniped at one another over inconsequential matters, and we began to avoid one another's company instead of relishing it. It was obvious that Gaston regretted taking me so deeply into his confidence, and resentment and distrust began to build between us. Late on the eve of Walpurgisnacht after we had both retired, I returned to the library, unable to sleep. I was returning to my room with the Epistles of Simocatta tucked under my arm when I ran into Gaston, who seemed upset at finding me still up and about.

"Falcone! What are you doing lurking in the halls like some thief in the night," he said.

"Lurking? I was merely borrowing a book to help me to sleep. When I first came to live here, you bade me treat your home as if it were my own. Your hospitality is lacking of late, Gaston, if walking the halls at night and reading your books is grounds for such accusation. Perhaps you'd best be off to count your silverware!"

"For months you have dwelt here, Falcone, eating the food from my board, drinking my cellar dry, and enjoying the comforts of my estate. If you are not finding my hospitality to your liking you need not suffer it a moment longer."

"I can see that I have overstayed my welcome," I said, stiffly. "In the morning I shall rid you of the burden of my company, and of the burden on your larder."

"In that case, monsieur, I shall bid you adieu," said Gaston, who turned abruptly and stalked off to his chambers without another word.

I was true to my word, and dawn's first light cast the Comte's estate in my shadow as I headed east on the road to Luxembourg. I felt a twinge of regret as I put Reims to my back; not for the loss of the comfortable life at Gaston's estate, but for his company. I truly valued his friendship, despite how it ended, and friendship has never come easily to me. I was ruminating on my loss when, later that morning, I was overtaken on the road by a mounted company of men-at-arms bearing the cotte d'armes of Reims. The sergeant pulled his horse in front of me, blocking my path.

"Pardon, monsieur, but the Comte commands your immediate return to his estate to answer charges of theft," the soldier said.

"Theft? Has some of Gaston's cutlery come up short after all?" I said with a smirk.

"No, monsieur, it was an item of a personal nature, and the Comte said that only you knew its location."

"And if I refuse to accompany you?"

"Then we shall drag you back by force."

I could see that the sergeant relished an excuse to humiliate someone above his station, so there was nothing else for it. I sighed and drew my poignard.

When it was over I sat down in the ditch to catch my breath and watch the flies, which were already gathering on the corpses that littered the road. I wiped the sweat from my brow and glanced up at the late morning sun, which was already making good on its promise of afternoon heat. Killing was such thirsty work. I pulled a silver flask from my tunic and paused to admire its intricate filigree, before unstopping it. Then I put it to my lips and drank my fill.

CONTRIBUTOR BIOGRAPHIES

MATTHEW BOTTIGLIERI lives in Portland, Oregon with his lovely wife Jen and three cats. When he's not writing, Matt enjoys studying Brazilian jiu-jitsu, guitar, and spending time with friends and family.

LISA BUCKLEY is a palaeontologist at the Peace Region Palaeontology Research Centre in Tumbler Ridge, British Columbia, and is currently working on her Ph.D. Tales of horror, hauntings, and the paranormal were an everyday part of Lisa's education growing up in southern B.C. She spends the summers in the wilderness with her husband, stalking the ancient denizens of B.C.'s prehistoric past, and the winters publishing the results under the constant supervision of her Maine Coon cat, Maia, while drinking endless quantities of Earl Grey tea.

You can read about her adventures in the field on her blog (http://shamanoftheatheisticsciences.blogspot.ca/)

ALEX J. CHRISTY was born in the suburbs of Los Angeles, California. As a kid, Alex found himself drawn to horror and fantasy, particularly the pulp stories of the 1920's and 30's. While most kids were thumbing through Goosebumps, he was reading about the whistling things that inhabit the remote mountains of Antarctica. As time went on his love of reading strange fiction turned into a desire to write it, and the influences of Lovecraft, Lieber and Howard found their way into his weekly roleplaying group. Last year Alex made the leap into professional writing and his first published short story, The Eye of Hytuuzsh, can be found within the pages of Libram Mysterium Volume 1. Alex also has a writing blog (www.themagneticstrange.com) that features his serialized fantasy/detective novel Save Versus Death.

Alex lives in Los Angeles with his beautiful fiancée Lisa and their orange tabby cat, Rusty.

ALASDAIR CUNNINGHAM was born in Scotland and raised in KwaZulu Natal, South Africa. He writes radio theatre, background and character stories for Bushido - the game. He lives with his wife and son in Cape Town, South Africa.

GARNETT ELLIOT lives and works in Tucson, Arizona. Most of his published work has been in the crime and pulp genres, but he has had fantasy stories appear in Libram Mysterium (Volume 1), Beneath Ceaseless Skies, Heroic Fantasy Quarterly, Swords and Sorcery Magazine, and the Eldritch Dark. You can follow him on Twitter @TonyAmtrak.

JOSH GRABOFF holds an MA in Medieval Studies from Boston College. His stories have previously appeared in Libram Mysterium Volume One.

S.M. OKEYB is an enigmatic man of the American South whose existence is merely suspected.

MARY QUIJANO is a public school teacher on the big island of Hawaii as well as published writer. She has several novels and short stories available on smashwords.com. Mary enjoys long board surfing, snorkeling and hiking in paradise, when not writing or teaching.

SEAN P. ROBSON is a palaeontologist with a Ph.D. in Geological Sciences from the University of Saskatchewan. When not studying the chitinous, scaled, fanged, tentacled and multi-appendaged monstrosities that haunted Earth's distant past, he writes dark fantasy fiction while listening to Dead Can Dance and drinking way too much coffee. He also sometimes blogs about writing, and things that amuse and annoy him at (www.seanprobson.blogspot.ca).

www.ingramcontent.com/pod-product-compliance
Lightning Source LLC
Chambersburg PA
CBHW070224140626
46555CB00018B/1264